4-11-18

A KILLING AT LYNX LAKE

BOOK THREE

OF THE ARIZONA THRILLER TRILOGY

SHARON STERLING

Copyright © 2017 Sharon Sterling

Changing Lines Press LLC
First Edition

ISBN: 978-0-9969408-2-5 (print)

Cover design by Karen Phillips
www.PhillipsCovers.com

ACKNOWLEDGEMENTS

To my editor, Priscilla Barton, my sincere appreciation for your expertise in the art of story telling and your support in the creation and evolution of this book.

Thanks also to members of the Tucson Sisters in Crime Old Pueblo Chapter for their comradery in the exhilarating process of authoring mystery/thriller novels.

Prescott residents Sally Jackson at Embry-Riddle Aeronautical University and Russ Miller, with Prescott's "Ask a Librarian" service were of great help in setting the scenes for this story.

To Diane Stanard, book lover and friend, my thanks for your enthusiasm and appreciation for this project .

I also extend my thanks to Al Lodwick and Ron Smith. Their books provided background detail during my efforts to bring Arizona locations to life. *Highlights of the Highlands Center and Lynx Lake Area of Arizona* by Al Lodwick and *A Guide to Prescott and Central Highlands Trails* by Ron Smith were authentic and valuable resources.

DEDICATIONS

* William T. Hickey, advisor and friend.

* Doctor Christopher Puca, a most compassionate man, the healing angel of Tucson, Arizona.

Chapter One

It was just a walk through the park on a spring day, a harmless activity prompted by ordinary decisions. The day felt made for optimism, the kind of day in which life affirms itself, in which death can play no part. It never crossed my mind I would get tangled up in another murder.

It was cool for early May at five thousand feet in elevation but I had my favorite sweater and thoughts of gardening to keep me warm. I was on a mission to put my hands in good clean dirt again. We power-walked that sun-illuminated spring morning, the big dog and I. Sounds of birds chirping and children laughing on the playground accompanied us. They were my two favorite choirs, singing rounds of the same joyful song. I smiled as we walked, approving of my own renewed cheerfulness. Optimism is a quality clients value in their psychotherapist--in me, Allie Davis.

I'll admit I was working at it, working to recover from the first killing, the one in Yuma. Grief over the loss of my best friend was bad enough; then there was the guilt. My younger friend, Kim, almost died because of what I did there.

Here in Prescott, Arizona, I expected to have a normal life. The Chamber of Commerce calls Prescott "Everybody's Hometown." Of course, that's just clever advertising but somehow it swayed me, contributed to the hope I might find a kinder perspective on myself here--a kinder perspective on the whole human race, for that matter.

The dog walked sedately beside me on leash, matching my quick pace with an effortless gait. I wondered if he was bored. As a veteran of canine search-and-rescue missions, he had experienced outings much more exciting than a walk through the park. Zayd is a serious-looking dog, so our progress wouldn't be delayed by casual dog petters, grabby kids, or cooing old ladies. *Old ladies, hah!* On the far side of fifty, I'm nearing that category myself.

Kim's dog was wonderful. I always thought people who preferred animals to humans were wounded souls, but after the perversion and malevolence I witnessed in Yuma, it occurred to me that this dog might sway my own soul to a prejudice for the so-called lower species.

We entered High Meadows Park at around nine a.m. The Park is a unique five-acre sanctuary. In addition to the community gardens, it features wildflower meadows and winding gravel pathways with gabion benches placed at strategic intervals. I bypassed all the distractions and led the dog straight for my raised vegetable garden, one of forty shared by a diverse group of Prescott residents. Only one other gardener worked her plot that morning, a young woman who waved with a friend smile as we passed.

My raised garden bin lay farther on, near the fence on the south-east edge of the one-acre plot, where it got both morning and afternoon sun. A few yards away, along the southern boundary of the park, a wooded area stretched about a mile and a half long and half a mile wide. To the east, across its narrow width, lay Watson Lake.

Earlier that week I had planted lettuce, zucchini and tomato seeds in my large bin. Other gardeners might start with young plants but I craved the ancient wonder of placing a tiny, dry, object into ordinary dirt and watching something green and alive spring up.

At the gate I was about to tie Zayd to a bench. Dogs aren't allowed in the food-garden area. I hesitated. He hated being on leash. Wouldn't it be nice to let him trot into the woods to explore a little and pee in private? I looked into his brown eyes. "Okay, Mister Dog," I said, "Kim trusted me enough to ask me to doggie-sit you so you have to be good. I could tell you to *stay*, but then you'd sit there like a statue. How about *stay close*?"

He cocked his head at the unfamiliar words. His collar was so loose I could have slipped it over his head but I unhooked the leash instead. He shook himself, jingling his collar tags, savoring his unexpected freedom then loped into the forest of pinyon pine and oak. Well, the leash and collar were there just to guide him, not control him. Kim's intelligent Black Lab and Rottweiler mix weighed almost a hundred pounds. He was big enough for me to pet without stooping and he had a mind of his own. He could not be bullied into obedience. His humans requested it with respect and he gave it with dignity and good grace.

Inside the garden, I found my lettuce had sprouted. I touched the tiny green leaves with a finger tip. Pathetically happy, I entertained visions of colorful, nutritious salads for my friend Betty and myself and baskets of excess produce I would donate to the food bank. I decided spices would occupy the other half of the bin. I began to sort through packets of seeds.

An unexpected sound stopped me. It sounded like a scream. So out of context, it couldn't be. Probably a child, playing.

Several more peace-filled minutes. Then another sound from farther away but unmistakably a woman's high-pitched shriek, ripe with horror. Oh, where was Zayd? I dropped the seed packet and turned toward the woods. "Zayd, come!" No response.

I grabbed his leash and went to the fence, slamming the gate closed behind me. In seconds, he emerged from the underbrush. I ran to him and hooked the leash to his collar while he turned his head toward the sounds in the woods. Another scream--fainter, intense, abruptly cut off. It triggered an ancient and instinctive surge of adrenalin, a ripple shooting from my core to the top of my tingling scalp.

I glanced down at the dog. His ears perked, his back and legs went stiff. He lifted his head. His nose made inquiries in the air. Then he looked up, locked eyes on mine, looked back toward the woods then at me again. That was clear enough. He wanted to go investigate. I didn't.

I reached into my shoulder bag for my phone to call 911. The touch of my finger brought the screen to life. I noted the date and time but then hesitated. What would I say? *I heard screaming.* "Where?" *From somewhere in Watson Woods.* "That's a big place. Where, exactly?" *I don't know.* "What did you see?" *Nothing.* "Who was it--who screamed?" *I have no idea.*

Damn. A call like that wouldn't help. Maybe there was someone closer who saw or heard her, someone else who would respond.

Zayd had taken a few steps forward, drawing the leash tighter, intensifying my indecision, my self-questioning. I had always identified my personality with the helping quality of my profession. Had the murder in Yuma drained me of compassion? Had it made me so frightened or so jaded I could ignore a cry for help?

I took a deep breath. Decision came on the exhale. "Okay," I said to the dog. He leaped forward so quickly it almost caught me off balance. Off we went, running down the path alongside the woods.

4

Now I couldn't take it back. Soon, in spite of the coolness of the day, I had to switch hands on the leash to swipe my wet palms against my jeans. There was nothing I could do about the cold sweat trickling down my back. Except endure it.

Chapter Two

Zayd's leash was fully extended, almost horizontal between my hand and his neck. His gait was a rapid trot, mine a flat-out run. Without a pause, he raised his nose again to sample the air. He knew where he was taking me.

I'm in good health for my age and slender enough, but my body had adapted to the almost sea-level altitude in Yuma. Prescott is a mile higher. After six or seven minutes at a flat-out run, I needed to slow down and catch my breath.

Just then, Zayd veered off the path into the woods, forcing me to dodge shrubs and leap over rocks and fallen branches. It was colder and darker here, where deeply shaded hollows still held crusts of snow. I heard leaves rustle, small branches snap under our feet, yet the noise of our passage still seemed muffled, unrelieved by the chirp of birds or other sounds of life. It felt as if invisible hands had cupped over my ears.

One second I was running, the next second I pitched to the ground on my knees and palms, still clutching the leash. It jerked poor Zayd to an abrupt halt. He glanced back at me for a second then turned forward again.

What had I stumbled over? Panting and in pain, from my hands and knees, I fell back onto my butt. I looped the handle of the leash over one sneaker. I tried to catch my breath and brushed at bits of forest debris clinging to bloody abrasions on my palms. Then I pulled up the jeans on the leg that hurt most. My right knee was badly scraped.

I needed another minute to regroup, but Zayd strained forward, his leash tugging on my foot. I reached down and tugged back. He turned, gave me a look of disapproval, then without further warning lowered his head, twisted his neck and jerked back. His collar slipped over his head.

That quickly he was free. That quickly he ran. In seconds he was out of sight in the undergrowth. I stared at the leash and empty collar, stood and gathered them in my shaking hand. I couldn't move one more step. I leaned over, placed my bruised hands above my knees for support, let my head droop and eyes close.

I straightened, with near-unconscious intent. I had to go after Kim's dog. I turned, trying to reorient myself, figure out where I needed to go. The screams had probably come from near Watson Lake. That's where I would find them, Zayd and the woman we had to help.

A few tentative steps told me my knee wasn't seriously damaged. I headed for the lake at a trot. My jeans rubbed against raw flesh with every stride. In less than five minutes, I reached the shore. Granite boulders and rocks of all sizes, from twenty feet-tall behemoths to pebbles, lined the water's edge. The expanse of blue shone mirror clear. A few ducks floated lazily on its surface. The dog was nowhere in sight. I called his name, hoping to hear a responding bark. Nothing. Shading my eyes with my hands, I scanned the shore slowly, methodically. No sign of him. My hands came down in slow defeat. I blew on my palms to ease the sting of abrasions, then leaned back against a boulder. *What now?* I realized how overheated I had become. I took off my cardigan sweater and tied the arms around my waist

The sound of a sirens drew me upright. The wail grew louder, reached a crescendo, faded to a whine and stopped. An ambulance? If the screaming woman was hurt, expert help had just arrived. I looked at my watch. It couldn't have been more than ten or fifteen minutes since Zayd launched us on this bewildering chase. I turned and headed back into the woods. I was almost halfway to where they ended when I heard a man's voice, a shout, then a dog barked, one short yip.

"Zayd!" I yelled and broke into a run.

I saw the policeman just as he saw me. "Hey, you, stop!" His hand darted to the butt of his holstered gun.

I was paralyzed. My hands raised slowly then, in reflex at sight of the gun. The officer approached me. I suddenly felt foolish and melodramatic, like a bad actress in a bad movie. My arms lowered of their own accord.

He demanded, "Was that your dog? What's he doing loose?"

"Not on purpose. It was an accident. Did you see where he went?"

The Prescott policeman didn't answer. He openly inspected me while I inspected him. The gun lay against his right hip, tucked into its black leather holster. His uniform was dark blue, the shirt long-sleeved, with epaulets on the shoulders and two breast pockets with buttoned flaps. Pinned above one shirt pocket was a gold colored badge and over the other pocket, a name tag.

I said, "Officer Benson, I apologize about the dog. I've been trying to catch him."

His hand moved from the butt of his gun to swipe beads of sweat from his forehead. His breath came hard and fast, as if he had been running, too. He demanded, "What are you doing here? This is a crime scene."

A crime scene? The woman had been hurt! I turned to look around. Nothing unusual--unless it was the shapeless mound on the forest floor about fifteen feet away. Surely it was too small to be a person. I began to tremble, there in the pine-scented shade. I grabbed my upper arms. They felt ice-cold against my raw, hot palms.

The officer stepped close enough to challenge my comfort zone. He demanded, "Who are you? Show me your I.D."

I fumbled with the zipper of the leather bag I throw over my shoulder when I go on foot, then handed him my driver's license. I said, "My name is Allie Davis. I was with the dog at the garden back..." I turned and gestured, "...back there at High Meadows. I heard a scream. We came to see what was wrong."

"Did you see anyone else, any one at all?"

"No one. Nothing. I went to the lake to find the dog but he wasn't there. Before that it was just me and him, running."

The officer shook his head, as if to clear it. His expression went from intense or even pained to a blank mask. He inspected my license, pulled out a note pad and copied information, then handed the license back. He said, "Well now I want you out of here. You and the dog. He'd better not come around here again. Someone might shoot him."

"Shoot him! I...."

He interrupted, "Go back to the path. Leave and don't come back!"

Horrified by his implied threat to kill Kim's dog, blood rose to my cheeks. "I will, but I have to find him."

"He's not here. He ran in that direction," he said, pointing away to where the path terminated at a residential street.

I turned away, telling myself that whatever happened to the woman who screamed, someone had taken charge now. Zayd was my primary goal. Kim had forgiven me enough already for what happened in Yuma. Our friendship wouldn't survive if I lost her beloved dog. I turned back toward the path, telling myself, *It's okay. I just have to find Zayd. I can't think about the woman. I won't think about her. I know nothing, nothing at all, about what happened to her in these woods.*

Chapter Three

I called Zayd's name as I walked but I didn't scour the underbrush, searching with my eyes. I knew that whatever I did, it was more likely he would see or hear me first. Still looking and calling, I arrived at the end of the path where it met the terminus of Oak Street. The ends of path and street formed a little cul-de-sac. A patrol car had parked there, its red lights still flashing, motor running. No one was inside. It must belong to the officer I had just encountered.

In the doorway of the home nearest the cul-de-sac, the homeowner stood, surveying the scene. Several others stood in the street nearby, obviously drawn by curiosity at the sound of the siren. I clenched my fists and cursed under my breath, ready to go back to the search, into the woods. Then I spotted someone I knew. For a confused second I wondered what he was doing here. Then it occurred-- why wouldn't he be here? Garvin was the oldest nephew of my good friend, Betty. He was the ex-husband of her niece. He lived just minutes away around the corner, at Betty's house, where lately he had become her caregiver.

"Garvin!" I called.

He turned around but hesitated. It looked as if he was about to turn away. I raised my arm and waved. He lifted his hand in a brief gesture and started toward me. I breathed relief.

An onlooker stepped aside for Garvin. He was that kind of man, in spite of his modest build and stature. Today he wore two-hundred-dollar Brooks Brothers jeans with a blue and yellow cotton shirt that had snaps down the front instead of buttons. He was bare-headed. His Ray-Ban Aviator sunglasses looked as if they were part of him. Hand-tooled leather cowboy boots completed his outfit. When I first met Garvin at Betty's house three weeks ago, I wondered about his style. Why hadn't he settled for either cowboy tough or GQ chic? His combination of both was a little off-putting.

He said, "Hey, Allie. What are you doing here?"

"Garvin, can you help me? I have to find...."

"Hey, slow down. What's got you riled up? You're sweating." He reached, as if to touch my face. I recoiled. I saw that instead of a watch, his wrist held one of those watch-cum-fitness bracelets, the kind that tell time, track steps and heart rate, do everything for exercisers except apply their deodorant.

I felt mildly embarrassed at my response to his gesture. I said, "I was at my garden when...oh, it's about Kim's dog. He slipped out of his collar and now I can't find him."

"Sure, I'll help you look. Where do you think he went? Maybe the lake?"

"I tried there, but...." I stopped. Just when I thought the day couldn't get any more bizarre, one of my new counseling clients, Chris Aren, appeared. He walked toward us, looking directly at me. If he greeted me, I would have to acknowledge him, but I would not 'out' a client, as such, by greeting him or her first. In a smaller town like Prescott, the stigma attached to mental health treatment and the clients who receive it is all too prevalent.

Chris smiled at me. "Hi, Ms. Davis," then he turned to Garvin. "Hey, Dad. Aunt Betty told me you were here. What's up?"

Dad? I forgot myself and the dog for a minute. The Father and son looked nothing alike. Garvin was about fifty years old, of average height, slender and wiry with tanned skin. His hair was long, salt and pepper in color, tied at the back of his neck. He could have been a model for the typical outdoors-man except for unpleasantly large, tobacco-stained teeth.

The differences between father and son were more obvious when they stood close. Chris is well over six feet tall with a strong-boned, athlete's body. His personality was cheerful and outgoing, like many athletes'. Nevertheless, during our two previous counseling sessions, I noticed something behind the affable exterior that didn't fit with the rest of him.

I looked from one man to the other, then saw the resemblance in their deep blue eye color and the width of their foreheads. Still, I couldn't get a similar *feel* from them.

I didn't notice Zayd until he was almost on us. I started. I took a step toward him but my relieved smile faded when I noticed his body language. He didn't wag his tail and show his teeth at me in a big, apologetic doggie grin. Instead, his nose scanned the ground side to side, then the air.

He came closer but not to me. He stopped in front of Chris and Garvin, sniffed their legs, circled them slowly, then collapsed onto his belly at their feet. He stretched out his front legs. He panted, tongue lolling and dripping. He looked up at me, obviously tired but satisfied, then cocked his head at me expectantly. What did he want from me? What was he trying to tell me?

A mixture of anger and relief pushed away the questions. They didn't matter. Relief won out over anger. I didn't have the heart to scold him. I had been clutching the collar and leash for so long I had almost forgotten they were in my hand. I slipped the collar over his head and tightened it while he remained perfectly relaxed. I turned to Chris and Garvin, "Thanks for offering to help me, Garvin. Nice to see you again, Chris, but I have to go now. I left my gardening tools back at High Meadows."

I gave Zayd the 'let's go' command. He rose and settled into a perfect 'heel,' walking beside me without resistance. It should have made me satisfied and relaxed, too. Instead, my mind was in frantic search mode over the dog's strange behavior. It was a lot like this when I was in session with a client, when I needed to grasp something very important about them but the insight wouldn't come. I looked down and began talking to the dog. "You can't do things like that when I'm taking care of you, Zayd. You're supposed to mind me and respect me. I'm your pack leader."

He glanced up at me for only a second, so human-like in his diffidence, as if he knew the absurdity of my statement. I smiled. "Well, Mister Dog, I'm still in charge here for the next few days until Kim comes to get you. No matter how special you are, I'm the boss and don't you forget it."

Back at the garden again, I wound his leash around a slat in the wooden bench before I went to retrieve my belongings, then returned to sit and take out my phone. Instead of making the call, I dropped the phone in my lap, leaned down, grabbed and held the dog's muzzle in my hand. I couldn't help smiling at his steady return gaze and the softness in his eyes. I said, "So can I get a little tail wag here?" He wagged his tail. Too cute. I had to laugh. Then I turned to the phone and called my friend.

She said, "Allie. What's up?"

"I have some concerns about Zayd but I'd rather hear about you first. How is your knee, and how is your father doing?"

"Is Zayd all right?"

"Oh, it's nothing. He's fine."

"Then my knee is a pain in the butt and I don't want to talk about my dad."

Kim's father was currently struggling with stage four kidney disease, on dialysis. "Okay," I said, "I'll just send lots of positive thoughts for him. So about your knee--what's the secondary diagnosis, *after* pain in the butt?"

"Torn meniscus. Only moderate cartilage damage but I can barely walk, much less run. It's killing me to know I can't take care of my own dog."

"Hey, stuff happens. Don't think of anyone but yourself for now."

"The surgery's set for Wednesday. Three or four day's recovery and I'll be able to walk--and drive. Then I'll come to Prescott to take him off your hands."

"Orthoscopic is amazing, isn't it?"

"I'm lucky it's my left knee. So what about Zayd?"

I knew the dog ranked high on Kim's list of loved ones, just below her parents, her brother, and her fiancé, Lon. "Oh. Well, today--it's a long story. The short version--he wiggled out of his collar and took off through the woods. He ran away."

"Damn! Didn't you call him back?"

"He wouldn't come."

"He wouldn't...." Her voice trailed off. "That's not like him. There was only one time I remember when...." Her voice faded completely. I sensed something important in her silence. I waited.

Finally, she asked, "Where were you when he ran?"

"We were in the woods. I didn't want to bother you with the whole story, but I think someone was attacked in the woods today. Less than an hour ago. It was a woman." Then I finally said what my gut had been telling me. I said the words. "Someone died there today."

In a flat, uncomprehending voice she asked, "What does that have to do with....? If he didn't come when you called, how did you get him back?"

"He came back on his own. I was standing next to a client of mine, the client and his father, and he just came out of nowhere. He ignored me at first. He circled around the guys then plopped down in the dirt in front of them. It was so strange."

"What do you mean plopped down?"

I described Zayd's behavior in more detail.

She said, "Allie, that was his 'down,' his signal that he found the person or thing he was looking for."

"I don't understand. Why was he looking for someone or something?"

"If someone died there...Allie, he knows about death. He's a rescue dog. He's been cross-trained. He finds dead people or sometimes live people. He finds things with blood on them or things with people's scent."

I remembered the police officer's yell and Zayd's bark when I neared the crime scene. I said, "It might have been her...her body in the woods. There was no one there but me and the officer. Benson, he said his name was. He chased Zayd away."

"Of course they wouldn't want a dog there. But if Zayd was searching and then did a 'down' it means he found what he was looking for. I wonder what or who he got the scent from. If it wasn't the victim it could have been the killer or an object the killer touched."

'Killer.' The word triggered a tremor deep in my core. I couldn't speak.

Kim said, "I can't believe he just took off on a find on his own. I've always been there to give him the scent object and the find command."

"I don't know what to say. I'm sorry, I...."

16

"Well, what ever. Don't apologize. He's safe now, right?"

"Of course. I'm really trying to take good care of him."

"I'll be there to get him on Friday. Probably Saturday. Saturday at the latest."

When we said good-by, it occurred to me again that Kim was confronting tough issues with her father's illness. I would support her as much as I could. As for my own little dilemma, her words offered reassurance. I loved Zayd, but my current dog-sitting days were almost over.

Chapter Four

I was at home less than an hour when Betty called, her voice thin and high-pitched. "Allie, there are so many sirens. Garvin told me there was some kind of accident down by the cul-de-sac. Someone got killed!"

I tried to lower and steady my own voice when I said, "You sound scared, Betty. You're at home, aren't you? Just lock the doors. I'm sure you're safe. "

"I'm worried about Garvin."

"Why?"

"I think he went down there. I don't like it but I'm not about to go down there myself to see."

"No, don't do that." For a split second, I wondered how much I should tell her. As little as possible. I said, "I'll go and see if he's still there. I'll send him home if I find him. Don't worry. I'm sure everything will be fine."

I put the phone down and rested my face in my hands. *Empty platitudes. Maybe nothing is fine.* I glanced at the clock. It was almost noon but it felt more like midnight. A touch startled me. Zayd had come to rest his muzzle on my knee. I patted his head before I grabbed my purse and sweater and went to the car.

At the cul-de-sac, two patrol cars and an ambulance lined the narrow road behind the first one I had seen. I drove around the corner, parked, and walked back. I didn't see Garvin but there were a dozen onlookers who stood or milled around, arms folded across mid-sections. They were eerily quiet, their eyes focused on the narrow dirt trail into the woods. One frowning woman murmured questions to another, who responded with a shake of her head. A man in a suit moved among them. He appeared to be

18

questioning each in turn, making notes on a hand-held electronic pad.

While I watched, a white sedan with a city emblem on the front door pulled up. Two men climbed out. One was young, tall and wore a camera on a cord around his neck. Most likely a crime scene examiner, I thought. The other man was gray-haired and stooped. A large case hung off his slanted shoulder. It appeared about to slide off. It was probably medical equipment. He must be the medical examiner. On his feet were heavy clod-hoppers. He walked as if he stomped across a cow pasture.

As I watched, the man with the i-pad approached and exchanged a few words with them. Then the two recent arrivals entered the woods.

The word surreal came to me, but this was very real even thought it looked all wrong; it felt all wrong. The patrol cars, the crowd of people, were out of place in this older neighborhood of stately, well-kept homes.

Some of the houses were typical, two-story Victorians with brightly painted gingerbread trim. Others were more contemporary craftsman-style but each displayed the unique personality of original architecture. With lovely green lawns and tall shade trees surrounding them, they exuded normality. A few days before when I walked down this street, waves of peace wafted over me. I remember thinking surely nothing shocking, nothing tragic, could ever happen here.

For some reason I started when I saw Officer Benson emerge from the woods. He spotted me, then went directly to the detective and said a few words, nodding his head toward me. He was talking about me. I froze. The detective looked at the small notebook in Benson's hand, then headed my way.

The detective's body was wide and solid, his face no less substantial. He had a short, hooked nose, small, intense eyes and a square jaw.

When he reached me he said, "Miss Davis?"

"Ms. Davis. Allie Davis."

"I'm Lieutenant Grozny. We need to talk."

"About what?"

"About what you and the dog were doing in Watson Woods."

I said, "Just walking. That's all."

Lieutenant Grozny was just a few inches taller than I, but something in his stance was as intimidating as the tone of his voice. "Why were you in the woods this morning?"

"I was walking--well running--with the dog."

"Where's the dog?"

"I took him home."

"Why were you running?"

"We heard the screams."

"What screams?"

"Three times. We heard a woman scream three times." My hands tightened into fists. My finger nails gouged the scrapes on my palms.

"What did you see?"

"I didn't...the only other person I saw was Officer Benson."

"Why did you let the dog go?"

"I didn't. His collar was loose and he managed to twist out of it somehow."

"Exactly where were you when that happened?"

"The dog isn't mine. I'm taking care of him for my friend Kim."

"You didn't answer my question."

"We were about halfway between the lower end of the Community Garden and here, on the path."

"You're from Yuma, Miss Davis? You're a long way from home. What brings you here?"

That's how it went. I seemed like an hour but was probably only ten or fifteen minutes. Finally, Grozny stopped pecking at the keyboard with one hand and closed his notebook. "I appreciate the information. We may want to see you at the station sometime in the next few days--or the next few weeks. Don't leave town." He walked away, leaving me with the empty, relieved sensation I remembered after vomiting. I shook my head to reject the comparison. It was a dark shade from my more dysfunctional past. I reminded myself of the reason I came--to find Garvin and send him back to Betty's house, to reassure her.

Just then, Garvin appeared, seemingly from nowhere. He stopped by my side and tilted his head toward the Lieutenant's back. "Quite a dick, isn't he?"

I nodded and tried to smile, then wondered if Garvin meant 'dick' as an insult or just another name for detective. I had already noted Garvin's penchant for double meanings. I said, "Betty is worried about you Garvin. Will you be going back soon?"

He nodded. When I turned to go, he grabbed my elbow.

"Why did he question you, Allie?"

"I guess they--I guess he thought I saw something--something to do with a crime. Do you know what happened?"

He shook his head and rolled his eyes. "The dick questioned me too. Walk back to the house with me. Betty is more upset than usual, isn't she?"

I didn't know how to respond to that. I had seldom seen Betty alarmed or excited without reason. In five minutes, we reached her modest one-story, three-bedroom home.

"There you are," she greeted us. "So tell me about all the commotion around the corner. Terrorist attack? Alien landing?"

Garvin brushed past her. "An accident, that's all, Aunt Betty. Don't get your knickers in a twist over nothing."

I bristled at his tone, but Betty didn't appear offended. We talked for a few minutes and before I left, I asked if she still felt up to meeting me for dinner tonight at Lynx Lake. She assured me she would nap and arrive at the restaurant on time and with a good appetite.

Reassured about her, I left and was almost back to my car when I saw changes had taken place in the drama unfolding at the cul-de-sac. The ambulance parked behind the two patrol cars had been replaced by a large van with a lift gate at the rear.

"Back, move back!" someone yelled. People near the woods shuffled apart, forming jagged lines on either side of the opening to the trail. Two overall-clad men emerged, carrying a stretcher with something wrapped in a green covering. The material looked stiffer than cloth. It revealed not even the outline of a body, yet I was sure the stretcher carried the remains of a woman, the woman who screamed in the woods.

I watched them load the gurney into the van and drive away. I stared after the retreating tail lights until they faded from view. A knot formed inside my chest. I fought the feelings. I refused to cry. My breath came quick and shallow. Zayd and I hadn't gotten there in time. No one was there in time to help her.

Chapter Five

The day--*that* day--wasn't over yet. Exhausted as I felt, I wouldn't have disappointed Betty by cancelling. She treasured every place she went, every pleasure she experienced because it might be her last, or the last one she could remember. At home, I showered, plastered a large bandage over the wound on my knee, drew on a pair of slacks and topped it with a linen blouse. I arrived at the restaurant at six, a few minutes before her.

Betty had been my friend for years, my mentor, the senior psychotherapist at the clinic in Cottonwood where we both worked before I moved to Yuma. Then a year ago, she called me to say she had moved to Prescott to take care of her ailing sister and would start a new, part time counseling practice. It sounded just like her, as compassionate and caring in her personal life as in her profession. We kept in touch every few weeks by phone. Seven months later, she called to say her sister had died from heart failure and she herself had just been diagnosed with Alzheimer's. She was sixty-eight. It was the first time I ever heard her cry. It was the first time, ever, I felt sorry for her.

Business was relatively slow this early in the tourist season at Lynx Lake Cafe. I was able to get a table by the windows where I could see hummingbirds working the feeders outside. Only a few die-hards were still at it as dusk settled over the forest, but I immediately saw a broad-tail and an annas. Too bad there was no direct sunlight to ignite their colors, but I heard the whirring of their wings and the high-pitched *chip-chip* sounds they made as they chased each other from the feeder. Some Native American tribes view hummingbirds as symbols of joy. I needed a bit of joy just then. At the other end of the large room, a hard-wood fire glowed in the stone fire-place. Settling back in my chair, I caught the scent of wood smoke. When I closed my eyes, I imagined a camp-out with all the charm of the outdoors.

This was not only a unique venue, it was a favorite place for wonderfully authentic German cuisine. Located about eight miles out of town down a winding rural road, the small frame building sat in a clearing among hundred-foot-tall pine trees, disguising itself as a strange little bait and souvenir shop. The entrance to the restaurant was through the shop, where an amazing collection of useful items like fish-bait and lures sat on shelves among whimsical, arcane or even unidentifiable knick-knacks.

Beyond the windows and bird feeders lay Lynx Lake. The restaurant was built for viewing the lake but it and the surrounding ponderosa pine forest are more than a nature-lover's vista. They provide habitats for fish and abundant wildlife--deer, elk, cougar, brown bear and birds of all kinds. When the waiter brought me ice water with lemon, he told me the bald eagles still nested on the eastern shore of the little lake.

Betty arrived five minutes late, like a seasoned actress taking the stage, perfect-posture tall and slender in the sweep and flutter of a dress in muted green. Once, the color would have complimented the mahogany of her hair but now contrasted with its silver-grey strands.

I told her, "You look wonderful, Betty," while I hugged her close. I caught a remembered scent like patchouli incense, both subtle and complex. I kissed her cheek before I let her go.

"Did you have any trouble getting here?" I asked, then regretted it immediately. She had been here dozens of times.

She smiled at me. "If I ever head this way then forget where I'm going and end up in a bar on Whiskey Row, please take away my car keys." I laughed. She still exuded common sense and practicality. The waiter greeted her and handed her a menu. When he left she continued, "I don't think I'm that far gone yet. I think I'm actually better since I started that new medication."

"Wonderful."

"But I am forgetting things. Things I did just a few minutes before. Sometimes I repeat myself. It annoys Garvin when I say the same thing over and over or tell the same story two or three times."

In my experience with clients, Alzheimer's symptoms include confusion, perceptual problems, and lack of judgment. The disease impairs self-awareness and insight to such a degree that most victims are aware only of issues with memory.

I said, "We're all a little forgetful when we're older. Some memory loss is normal." As soon as it was out, I recognized the professional counselor in my tone. I felt a nudge of self-reproof. Was I being patronizing to a friend?

She said, "Yesterday I went out to get the morning paper and couldn't find it. I went back inside and there it was on the table. I had gone out for it earlier, but couldn't summon that memory to save my soul."

"Not a big deal. No harm, no foul, right?"

She didn't answer. In the silence, I noticed her troubled eyes. Her grey hair was styled in a simple chin-length cut that curved elegantly and gently around her face. When she bent farther to look at the menu, I saw she wore only one earring. That was not her style; it was evidence of her disease.

Finally, she spoke. "Forgetting reminds me of a cartoon I saw. An old man and his woman friend are taking a stroll. He says, 'My memory is getting really bad.' They walk on a few steps. The woman asks, 'How bad is it?' and he says, 'How bad is what?'" Smiling, she bent her head to examine the menu.

The waiter appeared again and we ordered. I watched Betty sweep her cloth napkin off the table and onto her lap with a flourish. "How is your garden coming along, Allie?" she asked.

"Some things have sprouted already. Won't it be wonderful to have fresh tomatoes in our salads and fresh herbs for cooking?"

"The tomatoes I buy in the store taste like plastic, so yes, we'll have some wonderful, gourmet meals together. If you can tolerate the dinner hour with Garvin."

"Why not? He seems very...."

"Oh, don't tell me you're attracted to him."

I had to smile at her expression. "I am still single, Betty."

She blinked. "Well, if he's attracted to you, I'm not surprised. The grey streak in your hair looks like a hundred dollar salon job, and you have such an aura of sweet dignity about you."

The compliment surprised me. It brought a sudden memory that made me smile.

Betty noticed. She said, "What?"

"Once when I was introduced to another psychotherapist the first thing she said to me was, 'I've always wanted big, brown, almond-shaped eyes.' For a second I wanted to apologize to her."

Betty laughed. "Oh, don't ever apologize for having something other people want."

After a moment of silence, I said, "Betty, please don't concern yourself about Garvin and me. I wouldn't complicate our lives by dating your nephew. He's here to help you. I wouldn't interfere with that for the world."

"He is my helper. I never expected it from a nephew and he's not even blood. Adult children usually get stuck in the caregiver role. Makes me doubly glad I never had any. I wouldn't want to put them through it."

"I understand. I wouldn't want that role for my son, either."

"I never thought of Garvin as the care-giving type but he reminds me of things, fixes things around the house, helps me sort out my paperwork, pay my bills. I expect he'll know when to back away and let me go to assisted living."

"I don't know him that well yet, but he sounds like a great guy."

"Some people think he's mankind's gift, as they say. Others are leery of him. Garvin is strange. It's like he's two different people and one of them is very charming. If he's captivated you, I can understand."

I snorted. "Ha. At this stage of my life, I'm in no mood to be charmed--certainly not captivated. When that happens, you forget about all you give up, all you give in exchange for someone to hug and kiss and say 'I love you' to. It's a high price to pay. Except maybe for the ones who have cats." I tried to soften the words with a smile. "Or dogs."

She searched my face. "That's a point of view I've never heard from you before, Allie. Just lately? Since your friend in Yuma was murdered by her boyfriend?"

"Since you mention it, probably. Hey, I even have issues in my relationship with a friend's *dog,* so let's not talk about men. As a matter of fact, Zayd reminds me of some men I've known. He snores, he belches, he farts and he never says excuse me."

Laughter lifted her chin and brightened her eyes. After a moment she said, "I'm not going to let you dodge the subject that easily, Allie. You never told me why you feel guilty about your friend's death."

"Not really guilty, I guess, but certainly responsible."

"How could you be responsible?"

"It's complicated." I hesitated, trying to sort thoughts from feelings. Betty shook her head at me. She wanted more. She could be relentless.

I said, "Okay. So, it turned out the man who killed my friend Cindy was a co-worker of mine. For weeks, I didn't have a clue. Then when I started to suspect him, I wondered if I was imagining things. I knew if I talked to him face-to-face about the murder, I could read him. So I fed him false information. I told him detectives knew who the murderer was and the judge had issued an arrest warrant."

"How did that harm your friend Kim?"

"I didn't dream it could. But since he was guilty, he panicked, took off for Mexico. When he tried to escape, his car--it is complicated, Betty, but he crossed paths with Kim. She's an EMT. He kidnapped her and almost killed her."

"Horrible! But I still don't get it."

"If I hadn't fed him the false information he wouldn't have run, wouldn't have come across Kim at all. Wouldn't have injured her. I was so doubtful of my intuition, I had to test him to know if he was guilty."

She nodded. "You've heard me talk about guilt. There's justifiable guilt and self-punishing guilt. Tell yourself what we tell our clients. *Let it go.* Stop doubting your intuition. Stop doubting yourself, period. It's unbecoming for a woman your age."

Unbecoming? My age? The words were echoes from my pre-teen and teenage years. Another buzz word, *ladylike* often followed them from my mother's mouth. I chose not to take offense. Betty was still my caring friend and mentor.

We enjoyed our food in comfortable silence. Over coffee and a shared dessert, I finally asked the elephant-in-the-room question. "Have you thought any more about moving to that retirement community?"

"Ah, Valle de la Vacas, the continuing care retirement community. I have thought about it but I plan to stay here in Prescott, even after it gets harder for me. I can afford to go into one of the local memory care facilities. Ha. 'Memory care.' What a pathetic euphemism."

"It's a well-meaning euphemism, meant to be kind."

She grimaced and said, "I guess they're about as *kind* in Prescott as anywhere else. Besides, it's more beautiful here. A lot cooler than Cottonwood or Yuma." She shook her head. "Prescott isn't what it used to be, though. All the rehab facilities popping up. The drug users and alcoholics are about to take over Courthouse Square."

The hint of intolerance shocked me. "Aren't most of them here just trying to recover?"

"On the other end of the spectrum, too many rich people buying property for summer homes, driving the real estate prices sky high, pushing the natives out."

I raised my eyebrows.

She said, "Prescott used to be so simple, so uncomplicated, a sweet little town. No more." She wadded her napkin and threw it onto her plate. "Did you know they had a drive-by shooting from a golf cart there?"

"What?"

"In Valle de la Vacas."

I laughed. She was joking.

"I'm not joking," she said. "Drive-byes from golf carts. When they drive real cars, they just aim and hope for the best because most of them can't see worth a damn. You've heard the expression *grand slam*? In the *Valle*, they confuse the brake with the gas pedal and slam into buildings. Reconstruction is a major part of the economy there."

It was an amusing recital, but I couldn't ignore its implications. "Betty, you sound downright prejudiced against the place."

"Okay, the people there are well educated and interesting, but they're stingy. The richer, the stingier."

"What?"

"They're stingy rich instead of really rich."

I didn't know what to say.

She leaned toward me over the table to explain. "The really rich don't live in retirement communities because they have three or four homes and enough servants to take care of them. The stingy, greedy rich live in places like *Valle de la Vacas*. They got rich because their bottom line is greed. They don't care about the rest of the world, the environment, other people, animals. It's always *what's in it for me? How can I get more, make more, have more?* They're tight. Tight as a frog's ass and that's water tight."

I laughed. Still, couldn't let her slanted perception go by without a rebuttal. "Don't they deserve their money? Didn't they get rich by working hard?"

"Ha. The kids at McDonald's work hard. So do the house-cleaners and construction workers. How many rich ones there? Don't tell me an education makes the difference. We both have Master's degrees in counseling social work, and we make--you make--less than a plumber or an electrician."

I nodded at the unpleasant reality. Her intellect was, in many ways, still very sharp although there was a disconnect in her logic, or at least in her words. She had seriously considered the assisted living community, which implied she could afford it, which then might imply she was one of the *stingy rich*, whom she obviously disrespected.

She sat back in her chair, an end to the tirade. Her mouth drooped into a tired line. I could feel as well as see her energy flagging. Before she faded even more, I had a few questions about the client who showed up on my radar this morning. Was it safe to talk about him here? I looked around. Sunday was a slow evening at the restaurant, just a few other patrons at tables some distance away, well out of ear-shot. Reassured about the issue of confidentiality, I asked, "Betty, do you mind if we talk a bit about Chris Aren?"

She reached across the table and took my hand. "I do love that excellent young man. And I appreciate your coming all this way to take over my counseling practice. There's no one else I would trust it to."

"Thank you, but your need happened to correspond with mine. I was feeling burned out at the mental health clinic, with all its demands. As for my social life back home, I was starting to develop carpal tunnel syndrome from playing solitaire."

"I don't believe a word of it, Sweetie. But if you ever decide my private practice isn't right for you and want to leave Prescott, you can close cases and transfer people. Gradually," she added, then sat back and sighed.

"Don't worry about me or the practice. It will all work out." It was an honest comment. Most of my new clients were troubled but not seriously mentally ill. Their concerns were certainly not life-threatening. Several were suffering from depression or anxiety and several had marital issues. A frequent challenge for me was to break through a client's defenses to the real issue. A perfect example of that challenge was the real estate agent named Beverly. Her love of gossip was a distraction from the conflict with her daughter that she needed to resolve.

My thoughts returned to the questions troubling me. I prompted her, "About Chris....?

She said, "When we reviewed the client files, I should have filled you in more. He's Garvin's son by Garvin's first wife. Garvin and she married just out of high school. It lasted about ten years. Then Chris's mother divorced Garvin and remarried. Her second husband legally adopted Chris, which is why his last name isn't Kastner."

"I wondered about that. I didn't know they were father and son until this morning."

She looked down at the table, at nothing. "I know it's not considered ethical to counsel your relatives. I would never even consider attempting to counsel Garvin, but Chris is a grand-nephew. I wasn't close with Garvin or Chris, never spent much time with Chris when he was a youngster, so when I knew he needed counseling I felt comfortable about stepping in."

"His diagnosis is mixed anxiety and depression but he doesn't present like the typical anxious *or* depressed person, does he?"

"He's used to hiding his emotions, what with his work for the National Transportation Safety Board and the teaching stint at Embry-Riddle. Come to think of it, I sent him to see a psychiatrist for medication. I don't know what he's on, but that could explain a bland expression. Too many meds can give that flat affect."

"Right." I wondered what Chris might have reason to hide, in addition to his emotions. I said, "From your notes, I don't get the idea of real anger issues--violence?"

"Chris? No. As a matter of fact, I wondered about the horrible evidence of violent deaths he saw in his work with the NTSB, at those crash scenes. I thought it might have given him PTSD. You know, from vicarious victimization, secondary trauma, whatever they want to call it these days."

It was a possibility I needed to mull over later. I said, "I have to ask about Garvin, too. You said some people don't like him. Has he ever been in trouble for, like, domestic violence, assault?" My voice trailed off at the last word.

"Well, certainly not that I'm aware of. Why would you ask such a thing?"

"Never mind, Betty. Just a random thought and a silly question. "

"Speaking of Garvin, something happened early this morning--something I wanted to tell you about. It seemed important. I was uncomfortable about it but I can't remember now what it was."

The silence lasted several seconds until she asked, for the second time in an hour, "How is your garden doing, Allie?"

Chapter Six

Late that evening, Garvin called to say Betty arrived home from the restaurant safe but very tired after our long conversation. He asked what we had talked about.

"We talked about you, of course," I told him.

"I am a sexy topic so I'm not surprised. But then, you are too. A female beast-master, walking around with that big hound."

I informed him, pleasantly, I thought, that Zayd was not a hound. We chatted a few more minutes before I told him I had to go, I was exhausted too and needed to sleep.

Instead, I sat on the sofa and looked around dumbly. My life, the future I had created in my mind and trusted to materialize some day was now defunct, replaced by all this: a small crop of brand new counseling clients, a friend who would need more of my support and attention every day, a different Arizona city to explore and a new apartment to fit into.

Back home, my life ran on smooth tracks. There, I had an unexciting but steady job, a few good friends, owned a lovely house and had developed a sense of belonging hard-earned in that dusty, history-steeped, old-West town.

This tiny bungalow on Cedar Street offered a bathroom with no bathtub and a bedroom the size of a large closet. Every night while I tried to go to sleep, I reminded myself I did *not* have claustrophobia. Zayd lay on watch just outside my door, reminding me of the mythical dog Cerberus, the two-headed 'dog of disaster.' It was not comforting. Perhaps I was just too negative and too imaginative. My earlier telephone conversation with Kim had opened a maw of unknowns about Garvin and Chris which gaped dark and large enough to swallow me. Betty's comments about my client and his father during dinner hadn't banished the sensation I was about to float right into the monster's mouth.

I washed my face and got into my pajamas. I went to the kitchen for the unopened quart of rocky road ice cream. I had a premonition I was in trouble when at the silverware drawer I took out a long-handled ice-tea spoon instead of a teaspoon.

The lid came off the paper carton easily. I licked off the circle of ice cream clinging inside the lid. The lovely stuff in the carton proved too hard to spoon out. I had to scrape the spoon across the surface in order to get a mouth full. Then many scrapes and many mouth fulls. I had learned the best way to eat ice cream to maximize flavor and prevent brain-freeze. I turned the spoon upside down so my tongue got the cold of it instead of the roof of my mouth. Zayd sat by the table looking up at me with those soft brown eyes, but I refused to give him a taste. Chocolate is bad for dogs.

My thoughts circled around to the morning, what I now thought of as the tragedy in Watson Woods. Kim knew her dog. They both knew about death in its more tragic manifestations. What did Zayd's *down* in front of Chris and Garvin mean? That one of them killed that woman? It was simply unbelievable. Maybe one of them had touched some object she touched-- or that killed her--or was involved in her death in some way I couldn't fathom. Garvin or Chris? They stood so close together that morning. Did Zayd mean to stop in front of just one and if so, which one? Or did he deliberately indicate both? Garvin *and* Chris?

The ice cream was softer now. When I reached down with the long spoon, smears coated my knuckles. I licked them off, then put my other hand across my mouth and nose for a minute to warm them. Good. No brain-freeze.

My memory flashed on Officer Benson, surly Benson, who hinted he could shoot a dog. He was there, near that pathetic mound on the forest floor so soon after her last scream. Oh. What if the patrol car with the siren wasn't his? Was he there before the screams--causing the screams? My imagination wouldn't conjure a picture of the violent act itself, or of the perpetrator, not even Benson.

And who was the woman? What brought her to the woods? What connection might she have to Garvin or Chris or Benson?

Another thought branched off. Garvin was Betty's caretaker. If he had done some horrible deed and they arrested him, it would leave her with no one to help her navigate Alzheimer's dementia. That was a new world for her, a new world of uncertainty and impotence.

I started to feel much too full. My belly pushed against the draw string of my pajama pants but I couldn't stop eating and the carton was half empty.

What about my client, Chris? During counseling, would I probe for answers to his distress to help him or to discover the worst about him? Might doubt or fear shadow every session? What if I discovered--or even truly suspected--he was the killer? Would I rat him out to law enforcement? I had never knowingly violated confidentiality by sharing a client's private information. The law requires a therapist to report harm *about to occur*, not harm that's already happened. Would it be a betrayal--would it violate the strict ethics of confidentiality to report a killer?

My spoon was near the bottom of the quart ice cream carton. What? Had I eaten that much? It was gone, but the questions remained, screaming in my head. Finally, feelings of being bloated and disgusted with myself overrode the mental noise. I gave up and went to bed. Later, when the ice cream came back up I regretted the pecans in it. Small bits of nuts hurt my throat. When it was over I felt better anyway, like I used to.

***

In the small office, once Betty's office, Chris took a seat on the sofa. Clients usually wait for me to start the conversation but I could see Chris had something to say. He asked, "How did it go with your dog yesterday, Ms. Davis?"

"We got home fine, Chris. And you can call me Allie, if you're comfortable with that."

"Sure. Before we start, is that your car outside, the yellow Hyundai?"

"Yes, why?"

"A fairly late model?"

I was beginning to feel a little put-off, but I answered, "Yes."

"If it's a two-thousand fourteen or two-thousand fifteen, it's been recalled."

"Oh. Why?"

"Airbag failure. Could be dangerous in an accident. Have you taken it in yet?"

"No."

"Here, I'll write down the web site so you can check it out. Then the dealership can help you." He took a small pad and a pen from his shirt pocket to make the notation.

While he wrote it occurred that in my experience with clients, this was an unusual dynamic. I said, "Ah, yes, you're a safety engineer."

He leaned forward slightly, with feet wide-apart and handed me the slip of paper. I realized my client made me feel small or maybe just crowded. His presence filled the room. His six-foot-three body conveyed a strong masculinity, yet around his eyes and mouth, I saw evidence of the vulnerable child he once had been.

When he sat back, he said, "I'm still not comfortable with this, you know."

Ah, here was my client. I said, "I know it's not easy, Chris. People in counseling sometimes feel worse before they start to feel better. It's part of the process."

"I've heard that. You know, there are two psychiatric social workers at Embry Riddle. I've never been to one of them, but they stay busy."

"Why is that?"

He said, "Most of our students are very bright but they're not immune from psychological or emotional issues. A few have Asperger's Syndrome."

"I've heard some people with Asperger's focus on an aspect of science or engineering."

He nodded. "I think that's true. It's also difficult for the women at Embry, because they're the minority-- about one to every four men. There aren't any sororities or fraternities, but they do have a women's group."

"I'm glad for them. So, then you understand that needing support, even if it means accepting counseling, doesn't indicate a lack of intelligence."

"Of course," he said. He folded his arms. I noticed his polo shirt hung on his frame. The flesh of his upper arms hinted that once-hard biceps were now under-used. He must have noticed my judgment. He said, "I've lost a little weight lately. I've been running more."

"Oh, you enjoy that?"

He simply nodded and brushed his hand through his hair. Even before the gesture, I noticed it was tousled but not styled that way. It was fine and sandy-colored, receding a bit in front, suggesting a future widow's peak. I coached myself to see him and his situation like I would any other client's but a small part of my mind resisted.

His personal history was conventional, at least after the age of fourteen or fifteen. He and his mother and stepfather moved to Prescott, where he did well in school, loved math and physics and played sports. There were no disciplinary problems, at least none he revealed.

I said, "If you don't mind, Chris, I'd like you to tell me a little more about what was happening in your life when you started to feel anxious enough to need counseling."

He hesitated. His face remained expressionless while he obviously wondered how to begin. I watched him stare upward at nothing, then down at his knees while he pondered my question. I pondered as well, remembering his history. Betty had told me he played football in high school. He was a defensive back who after a few semesters got tired of constant pressure from the coach to hit the other players harder. His mother told him he wasn't suited to the general aggressiveness of the game and urged him to quit. She feared he would be injured. It turned out basketball was a better fit for him. His skills on the court and a high GPA earned him a scholarship to Embry- Riddle, where he majored in engineering.

In his senior year, the National Transportation Safety Board scouted him. He went directly from graduation to work as an investigator of aircraft crashes. He became the junior member on a 'go-team' of three or four. He had told me it was tough work in many respects, but fascinating and fulfilling. He was doing his part to discover the causes of air craft crashes. Those findings might someday prevent similar accidents. When he joined the American Society of Safety Engineers, he felt his career was on track and relatively secure.

Finally, he said, "I'm not sure when it started. It seems like it just crept up on me. It started--maybe about three months ago."

That recently? I had vague mental pictures of Chris walking among twisted pieces of aircraft and strewn body parts. How could anyone do that for five years and remain stable and unfazed? I said, "Can you tell me more about your work?"

He gave me a knowing smile. "It's probably not as bad as you think. Sure, we had to see bodies, body parts but FBI and forensic teams did most of the human recovery and identification work."

"What was your part in the process?"

"Our main focus was the debris pattern, condition of the aircraft parts, evidence of fire or explosion, that sort of thing. A vital part of most investigations was finding and processing the black box."

"How long did you spend at the scenes?"

"It varied. For simple cases, a small aircraft and just the pilot, maybe only one day. For commercial airline cases, we usually set up a command post at a hotel nearby. Three or four days on average, for the go-team."

"Then what?"

"Back at Headquarters, the FAA provided transcripts of communication between the aircraft and the tower. We always reviewed those. But the black box, hard data from the cockpit, was usually the key. The reports took time to write, more time than we spent on the actual investigation. We had to draw inferences and reach conclusions. The reports sometimes made important safety recommendations-- like advising manufacturers to recall mechanical parts."

I said, "Sounds like interesting work." Suddenly, a queasy sensation hit me. Chris might not be a vulnerable PTSD sufferer as Betty suggested. Instead, this ordinary-looking man who sat across from me could be a modern-day ghoul who delighted in stalking scenes of violent death.

I kept my voice neutral when I asked, "Did you like the crash-site work more or the follow-up?"

"The site work was more intense. Just being on the team was exciting. We had to be ready to fly out to anywhere in the country on an hour's notice."

"Did you ever feel like there anything *too* challenging or unpleasant about it?"

"No. All the pieces to the puzzle were there on the ground. It was a challenge to find them, assess them and sometimes collect and transport them for more analysis."

Two vastly different conclusions hit me. Either Chris was a secret sadist who delighted in destruction and gore, or he was an intelligent but sensitive soul who valued work that traumatized him.

"Chris, do you have insomnia?"

"Sometimes."

"Do you have nightmares?"

"No. Well, when I was about eight or ten, I had what they called 'night-terrors' occasionally. Nothing since then."

"Do you ever remember details of the crash sites at odd times--sights or smells or sounds that come back vividly?"

"Like flash-backs? No, not at all."

"Will you tell me why you're on leave from the NTSB?"

"Family leave. Amy and I had a baby."

"Yes, you showed me a picture. He's a beautiful baby. He's about three months old now, isn't he?"

Chris looked down, then raised his head quickly. "I couldn't go back, that's all. I asked for an unpaid leave of absence and got it. Amy and I have the financial resources between the two of us to carry us at least four or five months more."

"And you're not teaching this semester?"

He leaned forward. His next words came out between gritted teeth. "I couldn't face teaching, either." In spite of the grimace, I knew he wasn't angry. He was embarrassed--and there was something else I couldn't identify. I said, "No problem, Chris. Anything you want to add that might help me understand better?" He shook his head.

"Okay. It's almost time to stop, but first I have an idea I want to run by you." He sat back again, relief softening his face and body.

"Chris, could you to take me through one of those investigations in a little more detail?"

"I--how? Do you want to read reports?"

"That might be good."

"You can find all the reports on line. They're public information. Or I could take you to the crash lab."

"Crash Lab? Where is that?"

"On campus--Embry-Riddle. It might give you a feel for on-site investigations."

"Why not? A little field trip."

Before he left, we arranged to meet the next morning at seven-thirty a.m. at the visitor center on the campus. I saw him to the door, my head still swirling with questions. Before I returned to my chair,

I went to the table in the corner to check my message machine. One call, from Betty, marked "Urgent."

Chapter Seven

I pressed the speed dial number for Betty. I held my breath. She picked up immediately. "Allie, they took him."

"Took who?"

"Garvin. I don't...." Betty's voice wavered. She cleared her throat. "Sorry, I'm upset. They knocked on the door a few minutes ago."

"Who is *they* Betty?" I waited for her answer while I told myself to be calm because Betty was not.

"Two men. I'm so upset," she said again.

"Of course you are. Who were the men?"

"They said they were detectives." A pause. "I guess they did look like detectives. Suits and ties. One showed me a badge."

"Did they say what it was about?"

"For questioning. What kind of questions, Allie?"

I thought I knew the answer but wanted to find out how much Betty was aware of. I said, "I don't know. Did they say he was under arrest?"

"Oh, no. Why would they arrest him?"

My heart rate slowed a bit. "It's just routine then."

"It happened so fast."

"You're not used to detectives knocking on your door, are you?"

"Of course not," she snapped.

"Would you like me to come over? I can be there by five-fifteen."

***

She opened the door at my third knock. "Allie, what a nice surprise."

"Not really, Betty."

"Oh." Her face was a slide show of emotions while she remembered. "Right." She turned to walk into the kitchen. Her cat, Mange, appeared. The cat's white coat was long, silky and pristine, as it was the first time I saw him, when I said to Betty, "There's a story behind that name." She had smiled but never explained. Today the cat purred and tried to wind between my legs as I followed Betty, making me pause with every other step.

We sat down at the table. She said, "There's something about Garvin I need to tell you, but for the life of me I can't remember."

"That he was taken by detectives?"

"Oh, no. I remember that. It's something else. Something before."

"You'll remember later. In the meantime, I'll stay with you until he gets back."

"I don't need a babysitter," she said, then turned and touched my arm with an expression of apology. "The police really upset me. I keep thinking there's something I missed, something I should tell you."

"Try not to stress about it. The more you chase a memory, the more it retreats."

She turned away and picked up a wooden spoon to stir something in a large sauce pan on the stove. It smelled good. She said, "I was making dinner. I shouldn't worry. Unexpected things happen all the time."

I patted her shoulder. "What's this you're making?"

She turned with a smile. "It's stew, my grandmother's recipe."

"Ah, gluten free, I'll bet."

Her hand paused in its circle around the iron kettle. "What?"

Betty hadn't joined the no-gluten, no-sugar cohorts yet. "Nothing," I said. "Never mind."

While she stirred and added another spice, she talked about the recipe and its history. I knew distractibility is a feature of dementia, so I took advantage of it. I helped her cook. We made thick slices of garlic bread to go with the stew. While we ate, I kept the conversation on topics other than Garvin. With the help of a sitcom on TV, the next few hours went by without a hitch.

It was almost nine o'clock when we heard Garvin unlock the front door. He stepped over the threshold, he pulled a cigarette from his lips, turned and flipped it onto the lawn. Then he saw us. His dark expression changed as if on cue.

"Allie, hi. You came to keep Aunt Betty company?" He walked over, pulled a small easy chair closer to the sofa and collapsed into it.

I said, "She called me, so I came. You look tired."

"Yeah. Talking to ignorant dicks for six hours does that to me."

Betty leaned toward him. "Garvin, why did they want to talk to you?"

He said, "It was about the woman who died yesterday. In the woods."

"Who was it, Garvin?"

He hesitated.

She persisted. "Was it someone we know?"

"You might have met her. Carrie Lougee."

"Oh, the poor girl. I know her. I spoke with her several times at Chris and Amy's house." She turned to me and said, "Before Garvin came, she was helping me with my bill-paying and banking. Such a lovely person, but very practical."

Garvin fingered the packet of cigarettes in his shirt pocket. He said to her, "They'll question Chris next."

"Why, in heaven's name?"

"The woman was their nanny. She took care of the baby that died, remember?"

Betty's face twisted and tears filled her eyes. "I remember. Oh, that was so terrible."

I moved closer to lift her hand from her knee and clasp it in mine. Its fine tremor communicated her distress. I said to her, "It's late and you're exhausted. Let's not talk about this now, okay?"

She glanced at Garvin, then back at me. Her face set in resignation. "You're right. Time to go to bed. *'Sufficient unto the day are the troubles thereof.'* That's from the Bible. I've had enough for one day." She rose and without another word or a backward glance, went to her bedroom.

I turned to Garvin. "I've never known Betty to quote the Bible."

He shook his head. "Outside," he said. Together we went to the front porch. I switched on the porch light while Garvin lit his cigarette. We sat on the old-fashioned metal lawn chairs Betty had outfitted with thick cushions.

"Garvin, why would police want to question Chris just because Carrie took care of their baby?"

He turned his head and blew smoke. "Their first baby's death was a mystery. A mystery *and* a tragedy. Carrie was part of it because she was their nanny. She found the baby dead in the crib. Chris's wife Amy was off on a trip--she was a flight attendant. Only Chris and Carrie were in the house. Carrie was a nice looking gal. A bit on the chunky side but young and attractive."

"What are you saying?"

"There was an investigation. They interrogated Chris and Carrie. Upshot was, they ruled it a crib death."

"Well, why not?" I repeated, "What are you saying?" He flicked an ash from his cigarette over the porch railing but said nothing. I couldn't drop it. I said, "That was about two years ago, wasn't it? Is Carrie-- was Carrie--the nanny for the new baby?"

"No. Amy quit the flight attendant job. She's at home with this one. Buddy, they call him."

"Then I can't see how the nanny's death would involve Chris."

He turned to look into my eyes, squinting in the dim light. He waved away a mosquito, tilted his head back and exhaled smoke into the darkness.

Chapter Eight

I found the Embry-Riddle campus easily. The driveway of the main entrance led straight as an arrow to a building that housed the Visitors' Center. The visitor parking lot was well marked and just to its left. Inside the lobby, two students sat at a reception desk ready to tour-guide prospective students and their parents.

It appeared to be an unremarkable academic setting until my curious eyes stopped at a bronze statue in the large bay window. It was a young boy launching his toy airplane, energy and excitement in every line of his face and body. The glory of flight. It was not a passion I shared, but the statue depicted it eloquently.

Chris arrived a few minutes later. He asked, "Would you like to look around the campus a bit before we head to the crash lab?"

"Sure. I'm interested."

He paused with his hand on the glass door. "The central campus is small by most university standards. Then there's the flight line, where we train student pilots. We share it with the Prescott Airport. Hey, we just ordered two more Cessna Skyhawk-One-Seventy Two's."

"Great!" I said, as if I was not entirely clueless. Outside, we headed down a paved pathway between buildings. He pointed out boxy, plainly constructed dormitories, the student union, and classroom buildings, obviously created with consideration for academic function rather than esthetics. This certainly was no history-laden, hoary venue draped with ivy.

Chris said, "The University is diverse. We have programs for Meteorology, Air Traffic Control, five

Engineering programs and the first College of Global Security and Intelligence Studies. The newest is a course in Robotics. One of the oldest is the program that trains commercial airline pilots."

"I thought most commercial pilots came from the military."

"Some do, but commercial planes are very different from military jets. The pilots and crew still need training."

I decided to ask what might be a sensitive question. "Didn't I hear that the nine-eleven terrorists learned to fly at Embry-Riddle?"

His discomfort was genuine and intense. "The Florida campus. We don't talk about it."

In the next minute I stopped short, overwhelmed by the sight of an enormous airplane propeller mounted on the facade of a three-story-tall classroom building. The blades were as tall as the building.

"Impressive, isn't it?" he said. "From a KC 97 Stratocruiser. We've come a long way since that monster lumbered through the clouds."

"How so?"

"NASA sponsors our intern program for space exploration. We have an aerodynamics lab, four wind tunnels and a propulsion lab fitted with a micro-turbo jet."

"I'm impressed. To tell you the truth, I'm also a little overwhelmed. This is so far out of my technical knowledge comfort zone."

"Let's just head over to the crash lab, then."

A three minute walk took us to a one-story, frame building on the west side of campus. Markedly dissimilar to the other buildings, it looked as if it had once been a residence.

"I have to get the key," Chris said. "It'll only take a minute," and he entered the building. When he came out, he led me around to the side and back a few yards. There, an eight foot tall chain link fence topped by a row of barbed wire guarded entry to the site, ten or fifteen acres of raw, unimproved land. The lab was not a structure, it was an outdoor venue, acres of debris from actual air crashes. He keyed open a padlock on the gate and we entered.

Instantly I thought of the FBI's 'body farm,' where agents and forensic experts, including coroners and crime scene techs, studied corpses in all stages of decompensation. Here, they studied bodies of dead aircraft. Our first dozen steps down a narrow, paved path revealed nothing. I asked, "Where did the wrecks come from?"

"Different places, mostly in the U.S. The University started to collect the debris years ago. Part of the safety engineering program."

I remembered my original purpose in this exploration and began to watch Chris closely. He pointed to an object on the dirt. "That's a bird-strike canopy from a military jet."

It was a thick pane, several layers of plastic rather than glass, inside a metal frame. It had been rendered completely opaque by thousands of cracks. Farther along, a small clearing among the cactus and creosote shrubs revealed a private plane. It lay broken in pieces. It looked so small, almost like a toy. Then I realized why. I asked, "Where's the tail?"

He gestured. The shattered tail section lay a few feet in front of the plane's nose. "They call it the scorpion effect," he said. "In most crashes the tail is forced forward but remains attached. In this one, the pilot came straight in, no spin, no flaps, high speed, high impact. The tail detached, flung forward by the momentum."

I had been watching him as he gave this explanation. His face and tone of voice remained calm, devoid of emotion.

"Is there a crash here that you investigated?"

"There is--a commuter plane. Happened in New Mexico three years ago. This way."

At a fork in the narrow path, we continued to walk side by side. I wanted to assess his body language and facial expression but I couldn't step off the pavement to get enough distance from him. When he stopped, I followed his gaze. I gasped, "Is that really a plane?"

Small bits of metal and plastic, none larger than a dinner plate, lay strewn over a twenty foot long trail, their original functions unrecognizable.

Chris said, "A Beechcraft One-Twenty-Five, Eight-Hundred-A. It held eight passengers and two pilots. All killed. The captain attempted a go-around late in the landing roll, without enough runway left. Pilot error. They're the worst because they don't need to happen."

I looked up at him. I detected no sign of excitement or heightened emotion, no aversion or attraction but perhaps a little boredom. Farther along the path, after we saw one more crash reconstruction I said, "Chris I appreciate your bringing me here. I've learned a lot but I think I've had enough." What I didn't say was that I was now reasonably satisfied Chris did not suffer from PTSD due to his work experiences.

***

While I drove back to the office for my first appointment, my mind darted from one question to another, from a speculation to a suspicion to a memory and then another question. It was all about violence. If Chris loved violence, he hid it well.

At the crash lab, I saw evidence of accidental violence but on Sunday at the park, deliberate savagery had encroached on my life once again. Why me, a lover of Mahatma Gandhi, Martin Luther King, Jr. and Mother Theresa? I often wished I had been a young adult in the early Seventies. I would have worn flowers in my hair, marched on Washington with placards reading *No Nukes* and *Make Love--Not War*. I would have raised my hand in the peace sign at every opportunity.

Stop lights and heavy traffic told me to calm down and just drive. Then I remembered that Kim once told me people either love life or love death. We both knew which we were. Then there are the jihadists, terrorists, serial killers, revenge killers, thrill killers and demented killers. It seems like death infiltrates every aspect and level of society. TV and film producers cater to millions of violence voyeurs. Even the fashion industry panders to death-lovers. Designers create all kinds of garments embellished with human skulls, the universal icon of death, death symbols on shirts, jeans, hats, even tiny onesies worn by tiny babies. Whenever I see one of those, I want to scream.

The angry protests in my mind became an audible reality--a siren. I glanced back, saw flashing red lights behind me. My speedometer said fifty-five. This was a thirty-mile per hour zone. I slowed and pulled over, still inwardly ranting about violence. As the officer got out of his car and walked toward me, I coached myself to let it go and resign myself to consequences. Just as well. The traffic cop gave me a scolding along with a ticket. The scolding left me deflated and the ticket made me two hundred dollars poorer.

Chapter Nine

My android phone said seven a.m. Wednesday. I poured kibble into Zayd's dish and poured coffee into my cup. It was the morning of Kim's knee surgery. I wouldn't call her until afternoon, when she had slept off the anesthesia. My first appointment of the day wasn't until eleven a.m. but after my half-hour walk with Zayd, I decided to go in early anyway.

The first thing I noticed was the message light on the office desk phone blinking, as I hung my jacket on a hook and put away my purse. It was Amy, Chris's wife. I didn't need to check my file for permission. He had already given me written and verbal authorization to talk with her.

In the office fifteen minutes later, she placed her sleeping infant in his little carrier at one end of the sofa and sat down at the other.

"Thanks for letting me come on short notice," she said. "I'm confused, I really am." She looked over at the baby. I looked too and instantly cherished the sight of him. He reminded me of my own son as a newborn. I could almost feel his silken skin, the warm tenderness of his tiny body in my arms. Of course I couldn't ask to hold him.

Amy wiped tears from her pale blue eyes then placed the tissue on her lap. With long, sensitive fingers, she slowly tucked her long blond hair behind her ears. "I love Chris so much but...." Her voice trailed from a weary whisper to defeated silence.

"I'm glad you came, Amy. What you tell me could help me help Chris. You know, everything you say will be confidential."

"That's what Chris said. He likes you. I feel like I can trust you, too."

"Everything you say is something I want to hear. But why don't you start at the beginning of your relationship with Chris, then your life together since you married?"

"He was so sweet. The nicest man I'd met in months--more friendly and more...human than most engineers."

"Oh?"

"I had already met a few of the other professors-- really cold, nerdy people. There's a saying that engineers are the dumbest smart people in the world."

"I've heard that, too. It's probably about having a superior intellect but a deficit in emotional intelligence. So, how did you meet Chris?"

"I was a flight attendant. Two others and I were on layover in Chicago. The hotel we used was the NTSB's temporary base during an investigation." She leaned back into the cushion and closed her eyes.

After a full minute, I wondered if she had gone to sleep. "Go on, Amy."

"We met at the hotel breakfast table. Over scrambled eggs and toast. Engineers aren't my favorite people, as a rule--so little emotional intelligence. I had never met one from Embry-Riddle. Chris was easy to talk to, bright and funny but also steady and solid. Just so warm and human. We got married five months later. We both wanted a family and he was making good money, so we got pregnant right away."

"How did it go?"

"No problems at all. We were so lucky. The birth wasn't bad, and Hailee was beautiful. Pink and smooth and perfect, no birth marks or blotches or bald head, just a perfect little miniature of a perfect person."

She pulled more tissues from the diaper bag on the floor. I waited.

"Chris was in love with Hailee. He'd hold her and walk around singing to her even when she didn't need to be held. He'd get up with her in the middle of the night so I could sleep, and when I went back to work-- when she was six weeks old--he took care of her. We had Carrie, the nanny, of course, but she told me Chris was right there whenever he could be. He would feed her, give her a bath, change her diaper."

She stopped again, and I thought I knew why. "Take your time," I said.

"I was on a flight when she died. Thirty-five thousand feet somewhere between Phoenix and Houston when my baby died in her sleep."

Her breath sucked in sharply. I waited. "Carrie found her. Chris was there too, but he had come in late the night before, from an investigation, and he was still asleep."

Her silence lasted until I prompted, "And?"

"They said it was a crib death. That didn't make it easier for us. It made it harder, because there's no 'why' or 'how' to explain it. It just happens sometimes, they said." She clenched both fists against her mouth. Her next words came out in muffled screams. "Well, *why* to *us*? *Why* to our beautiful Hailee?" Amy wiped her face and looked to see if she had woken her baby. He still slept soundly.

In the presence of such intense pain, I felt completely inadequate. Finally, I managed to whisper, "I am *so sorry* for your loss," but even as I said them, I judged the words useless and banal. How could I help? "Would you like a glass of water, Amy?"

"Thanks." She took the plastic cup and gulped water, obviously composing herself enough to continue.

"I didn't know how we could go on, but we did. Chris wasn't eager to have another baby, but I wanted it. After a year, we got pregnant again. You know, during those months we held each other a lot and reassured each other a lot, and read stuff on crib death and how to take care of a newborn. We already knew it, but maybe there was information we had missed?"

I shook my head. I doubted any words would reassure her.

"I thought Chris would be thrilled to have a little boy but he didn't even want to name the baby after himself. It was my idea. I insisted on it, but from the start, he wouldn't say his own name. He called the baby Buddy. We all do now."

"He's an adorable baby."

She continued as if the words hadn't registered. "I don't understand it, Allie. Chris is so different with this baby. He doesn't want to hold him, doesn't want to take care of him when I have to go out. Once, I asked him if he was afraid of the baby. It made him really angry. He just walked away from me." She looked away from me and lowered her head.

"What do you think that was about?"

"The truth is, we're both afraid. We're afraid this baby will die, too."

"Amy, that's understandable. It's a normal reaction in your situation. But don't you think it's an unrealistic fear?"

She looked up and nodded. "Maybe it was the fear that changed Chris. It started when he brought me home from the hospital with Buddy."

"I'm not sure what you mean. I understand he wasn't the same kind of father to Buddy. What else started? What changed?"

"For one thing, he started to run. He used to go to the gym to work out three or four times a week. Now he goes out any time of the night or day, without changing into his sweats. Lots of times he doesn't go to the gym, he just runs. He'll come back an hour or so later. He looks--not just tired. He looks relieved. Sometimes he seems--even defeated. I ask him what's wrong, but he always says 'nothing'. He's lost weight. He's not himself."

"He knows that, Amy. And he's working on it. I'm doing--I will do--everything I can to help him."

After she left with the baby, I had ten minutes to assimilate everything she had told me and regain my composure enough to greet the next client. He had told me he liked to run; it was part of his exercise program. Evidently, it wasn't that simple. What was he running from?

Chapter Ten

It always takes a few minutes after the last appointment of the day for me to come back to myself, to my own life. At five-thirty on the afternoon of Amy's visit, I sat down on the clients' sofa in my office to get myself back. I decided to call Kim, betting she had slept off her anesthesia enough to talk. I asked, "How are you doing, girlfriend?"

She laughed. "Girlfriend? You sound like an over-zealous millennial."

"I wish I was that young. I'm about to be pleasingly plump, wear purple, smell like peppermints and call everyone 'dear'. I already have the lace-embroidered handkerchiefs and clunky shoes."

"Ah, the perfect old White Lady. Well, when I get old, I get to have lots of wrinkles on my dark brown skin and be very wise, ha-ha."

"Okay, my Native friend, you win the aging game. So how is your knee?"

"Wrapped, swollen and painful. I'll be okay. How is my partner-dog?"

"He's good. I found a great canine day-care place. He likes it but I only left him there once. I had an extra-full day at the clinic and didn't want to leave him alone that long."

"He hasn't tried to run away again, has he?"

"That's what I wanted to talk to you about." Kim already knew about Betty and why I was here in Prescott. I quickly filled her in on my relationship to Garvin and Chris.

She hesitated. "Do you really think one of them murdered the woman?"

"After what Zayd did on Sunday and what I've seen and heard since, I think it's a possibility."

"Then you could be in danger there, yourself, Allie."

"Me? I can't see that."

"You counsel one of them and see the other almost every day."

"Well, Betty lives with Garvin. She's not afraid of him. I'm thinking other people here could be in danger--a beautiful little baby boy."

"Damn. You're in it deep enough with Chris and Garvin. I won't even ask how the baby comes into it. Okay, back to Zayd. You may be focusing too much on his 'down.' It could have been a coincidence, a fluke, nothing to do with the murder."

That stopped me short. I said, "You're the one who told me about the down--what it probably meant."

"I know, but...." I didn't say anything. Then she said, "Why don't you try this? Take Zayd and go back to the woods. Chances are you'll find a dead animal he smelled, maybe a female dog on the loose. He's neutered, but.... Or maybe he just wanted to run."

I was too tired to reason against her logic. "Yeah. Maybe I added two and two and came up with five. So, you'll be here Saturday?"

"I promise."

***

I had to admit that Sunday's clouds of shock and fear, along with my recent traffic stop, had pushed me into a dank mood. I knew I needed a re-boot, a re-wind of circumstances and observations. I headed out with Zayd soon after I talked with Kim, thinking her advice was good, but we took a different pathway through High Meadows. It led to a large patio surrounded by a white picket fence, bordered with flowering plants. The unique outdoor room held a bench made from the fenders and seat of a 1956 Ford. Just outside the fence, an ancient bicycle with a wicker basket on the handlebars leaned against a mesquite tree, exuding sweet nostalgia.

I tied Zayd to the trunk of the tree, made sure his collar was tight, and went to sit in a cushioned basket swing. I gave myself a push with the toe of my shoe and swung lazily back and forth while I watched the day ease toward evening. Several ornamental pear trees nearby were in bloom, their crowns of white blossoms as full and frilly as ballet dancers' tutus. A fleeting breath of subtle fragrance reached me while the swing's gentle motion soothed me and the lull of evening pushed away lingering forebodings.

My reverie didn't last long. I hadn't noticed the sun slipping furtively down toward the profiled peaks of the Bradshaw mountains. Their jagged black outlines scrawled across the fading blue sky, while gathering twilight backlit the foothills. The lower slopes appeared blanketed with the varied colors of Autumn--hues of scarlet, sienna and orange. They had blotted out the soft shades of Spring. The last rays of light stained the horizon with the hue of blood. I shivered in my cotton shirt. Time to go to the woods. We'd have to hurry before full darkness descended.

I abandoned the cozy swing and set out again on the path, keeping Zayd on heel beside me. Before we reached the spot where he had veered into the Watson Woods, we entered it again. This time I led the way over the uneven ground. After a few yards, I saw a deviation in the forest floor that struck me as strange. In the shadows of dying light, the groundcover appeared disturbed. I went closer to get a straight-on perspective. It looked like a path.

Zayd put his nose down and stepped forward. I tightened my hold on the leash and walked to the right a few steps, then left, past the original focus point, then right again. There it was, not a well-worn path, but a disturbed line, a faint trail through strewn leaves and pine needles. In my mind, I pictured the woman who created the path with her running feet, running out of the woods back toward the cul-de-sac. The mental picture coincided with the sounds I remembered. The second and third screams were fainter. She ran from her attacker.

I led the dog alongside the trail for five minutes or more. In the last of the fading light, I saw ahead of us strands of bright yellow and black, colors rare in nature. It was crime scene tape left behind, still strung between the trees.

I began to watch Zayd's reactions more closely. He didn't appear agitated but with his nose to the ground, he walked toward the tape. I followed. He walked under it and then I ducked under it. He stopped a few yards farther on, nosing the ground again. I squatted down to look. One large, black, clotted droplet on the ground and few muddy-looking smears staining oak leaves and pine cones. Blood spoor.

Zayd raised his head. I looked, then jerked upright. It was a uniformed police officer taking down the crime scene tape. He saw me. He muttered, "What the...?" then yelled, "Stop where you are. Do not move!" He threw down the roll of tape. His rapid stride brought him just out of Zayd's reach. The dog stopped at the end of his leash, watching, alert and watching.

I stared at the officer, the same one I had encountered on Sunday, Officer Benson, young, tall, slender, brown-haired, rather ordinary-looking. He demanded, "What are you doing here?"

62

I tried to make light of the situation. "I've already introduced myself. You're not going to pull your gun on me, are you?"

His scowl deepened. "Jokes about guns are never funny. You're trespassing on a crime scene. What are you doing here again?"

I managed to say, "Trespassing? I didn't mean to." The pitch of my voice sounded, even in my own ears, like that of a frightened child.

He was not satisfied. "I asked you a question. What are you doing here?"

His aggressiveness was palpable. It drew a growl from deep in Zayd's throat, a warning hum. I said, "What difference does it make? You were taking down the crime scene tape."

"It makes a difference if I say it does. Put your hands up. You're under arrest!"

Chapter Eleven

Under arrest! I raised my hands slowly, trying to fathom this bizarre twist of circumstances. "Arrest for what? I haven't done anything."

"Failure to obey a lawful order."

"Order? What order?"

"On Sunday I told you to leave and not come back. Criminals come back to the scene of the crime."

I stared at him, stunned by his hostility and the absurdity of his statement. He was serious. I looked over at Zayd and flexed the wrist that held his leash. "What about the dog? Is he under arrest too?"

Officer Benson looked at Zayd. Zayd calmly but intently looked back and the warning hum sounded again in his throat. The officer turned, his eyes boring into mine. He said, "Wrap the leash around that," and lifted his chin toward a young pine nearby.

I hesitated, then decided I didn't have much choice. I had to go along with this ridiculous situation. I looped Zayd's leash around the trunk of the tree several times, and moved away. Officer Benson walked forward until he was toe to toe with me. He said, "You are under arrest. You have the right to remain silent...."

I stopped listening to focus on bladder control. He was reading me my Maranda rights. *My* rights, not those of some drunken idiot stopped for DUI or someone caught red-handed in a burglary. This was beyond unreal. My heart raced ahead of his words.

The rattled-off speech finished, he said, "Hand over the purse."

I took the small leather purse from over my shoulder and gave it to him. It held only my smart phone, my driver's license, my house key and a tissue. He took them out one by one to examine each closely, then unzipped two empty compartments and explored them with his finger. "Do you have any weapons? Carrying anything that could hurt me in your pockets?"

He wanted to frisk me, damn him. I smiled a challenge at him. He looked again at my t-shirt, tight jeans and jogging shoes. Where could I be hiding anything?

The second he touched me, Zayd stood at alert. He remained silent while Benson ran his hands over the small of my back and then down my legs. He felt inside both my jeans pockets. From the right one he pulled out my bandana, then let it drop from his fingertips. I caught it in mid air. He all but flung the purse back at me. "Get the dog and move!" He gestured toward the cul-de-sac.

I unwound Zayd's leash and headed away, Benson close behind. He probably would have handcuffed me if not for the dog. Self-awareness returned slowly, the feeling of my heart beating like a frightened rabbit's. A few strides later I looked back to see the officer with his head tilted to the side, talking into a radio on his shoulder. One of his hands held the incomplete roll of crime scene tape; the other rested on his gun holster.

We walked. My heart slowed enough so I no longer felt I might embarrass myself by fainting. That definitely was not in my usual repertoire of behaviors. At the cul-de-sac, we reached the patrol car. The officer opened the rear door for me. I got in but when Zayd tried to follow, Benson closed the door on the leash, which left Zayd outside on a very short line. Benson walked forward and leaned against the front fender of the car ignoring the dog, who then ignored him.

Why didn't he put Zayd in and drive away with us? What now? I looked around the interior of the patrol car, relieved there was no Plexiglas or wire mesh barrier between the back seat and front to make me feel even more humiliated, even more like a criminal. In the next five or ten minutes, my imagination conjured scenarios inspired by TV and film. I had no personal frame of reference for arrest and incarceration.

In the gathering dark, a white van pulled up and stopped. A man wearing a one-piece coverall got out. Officer Benson opened the back door for me and said, "Get out. Give me the bag." Still holding Zayd's leash, I handed him my small purse. He threw it onto the front seat of the patrol car, then walked to meet the man, who held in his hand something that looked like a whip. In the dim light of an overhead street lamp, I spotted and read the small lettering on the side of the van, 'Animal Control.'

My heart resumed a heavy drum-beat. I blurted, "No, Officer Benson! He's not my dog but I'm responsible for him. Please he's a good dog. Let me call someone to come and get him."

Officer Benson whirled around. His arm shot out. His finger pointed at me. "Stay where you are!"

The man from the truck held a long pole with a loop at its end. He came toward Zayd very slowly. When close, he dipped the corded loop over the dog's head and tightened it in one swift motion. Zayd turned to look up at me. I tightened my hold on his leash.

"Let go of the leash," the man said.

"No. You can't take him."

Officer Benson leaned toward me. "Let go or I will add *resisting arrest* to your charges."

I considered it for a split second. Dark logic told me Zayd and I were no match for this legal aggression, no matter how unwarranted. I unclenched my hand. The leash dropped to the ground. The man began to drag my dog away, his leash snaking behind on the asphalt.

My dog. At that moment, he *was* my dog. I watched Zayd pull back against the pole and noose. He dug in with his feet, tossed his head from side to side, twisted his beautiful black body almost in half in his struggle against the assault. Officer Benson followed them. He unsnapped the holster at his waist and placed his hand on the butt of his gun. It hit me--if the dog managed to turn and bite either of them, he would shoot Zayd! I closed my eyes, clenched my fists and willed, prayed, sent the dog silent messages to surrender.

They dragged him to the van. It took both the officer and the dog catcher to lift him up. In a split second before he disappeared into the truck, he looked   back   at   me.   His   eyes!

Chapter Twelve

"Stand up."

I didn't hear the command.

"Get up!"

My legs had given way. I was on my knees, palms on the blacktop. I struggled to my feet and watched the Animal Control van pull away. When I couldn't see even a glimpse of red tail lights, I took a deep breath. I rubbed the dirt and pebbles from my hands. Zayd had been so brave and so smart. He had probably resisted a natural instinct to tear the two men to shreds. He had saved his own life.

I walked the few steps to the patrol car without a word, got in the open door and sat down. I told myself that at least he was safe, for now. I took the bandana out of my pocket and wiped my eyes and my forehead. I always carried one like it because those scraps of cotton evoked reminders of my grandmother, a spirited, strong-minded half-Cherokee woman known for both her wisdom and courage. She carried a red bandana and wore a small medicine bundle on a leather string around her neck. I wouldn't carry a red or blue bandana because they were associated with gang emblems, so mine were either green or yellow.

I thought about Grandmother's medicine bundle and wished I had one now. I expected the patrol car would pull away, siren blaring. Instead, when Officer Benson got in he took the driver's license out of my purse and began to write on a thick pad of paper. We sat in silence in the enclosed space. Darkness had drawn a curtain. A dim glow from the car's dashboard was the only light inside. I leaned forward to see what my captor was doing. Without turning, he said, "I'm writing the report now so you'll go right into processing when we get to the booking facility."

I had no idea what he meant. He finished writing, took the wheel and we pulled away to drive through Prescott. It was a different perspective, from the back seat of a police car, to view the little city and its people. I was grateful for the dark. No one could look back through the window and know it was me.

He pulled the patrol car up at a one story brick building. It and the parking lot behind it were brightly lit, like a venue for happy celebrations. The word 'surreal' came to me. I started to open the car door but there was no handle. Right. Officer Benson got out, walked back, opened the door and grabbed my upper arm. I resisted the urge to jerk it away. We walked into the building like that. I felt about ten years old, being dragged to the principal's office.

We entered a small reception room where a uniformed officer sat at a computer. He glanced up, nodded at Officer Benson then returned to his work without a glance at me. On the door ahead was a key pad. The officer punched in a code and we entered a large room separated into work spaces with shoulder-high divider panels. A man in a uniform different from Prescott blue walked toward us. This officer's shirt was tan, his slacks brown. His skin was a deep, tanned color with a hint of ruddiness which told me he was Native American.

The Officer nodded at him then said to me, "This is the Yavapai County booking facility and this is Deputy Wall, one of the detention officers. He'll process you." He handed the deputy my little bag and the papers he had filled out in the car then simply walked away.

Process me? I imagined myself like a side of beef dissected into many cuts. The deputy threw my bag on a very battered metal desk, motioned me to a chair beside it and sat down without a word. He took a blank form from a pad on the desk and began to copy information from the Prescott police officer's report. He looked up to ask, "Yuma? Is that your current address?"

"I live here now." At some point while I recited my contact information and other details, I felt my angry flush begin to cool. I thought about Zayd again, where he was, how confused and frightened he must be. I determined not to cry. My staunch, spirited grandmother would not have.

The deputy put down his pen, pushed away from his desk and stood. He said, "Time to take your picture." Then he looked down at me. "Uh.... We can't take your picture when you're crying."

I had not uttered a sound, but hard-fought-against tears streamed down my face faster than I could swipe them away. I looked up. "Then I suggest you break for coffee, deputy, because I'm not an actress and I don't start or stop crying on cue."

"We can do fingerprints next."

"When can I go get my dog?"

"What dog?"

I counted silently, actually started to count to ten rather than explode in rage. At the number seven, I realized that in spite of having read Benson's report, this man didn't know all that had just happened to me and the dog. I began to explain. "Zayd belongs to my friend. He's trained to rescue people."

He said, "Active? Where does he work?"

"Yavapai County Search and Rescue."

He listened with an immobile face while I added that I had responsibilities to my Apache friend's dog, I had clients to see tomorrow, and responsibilities to my friend with Alzheimer's Disease.

Deputy Hall nodded, apparently unfazed.

My fist clenched around the bandana in my pocket that reminded me of my grandmother, that reminded me to be strong. I asked, "What happens next? After the fingerprints and the photo?"

"Retina scan, DNA swab, full body search."

"A strip search?"

"A female deputy on duty. You'll surrender personal items along with your clothes. She'll issue you a uniform. While she's doing her thing, I'll check the data base for outstanding warrants. Then we'll do a health screening."

"For the love of.... I am healthy. I don't need to be screened."

"That may be. Some people who come through here are HIV positive, have TB, or maybe just a bad case of lice. Screening is for your protection as well as ours. When we're done you'll go to the holding cell and wait for the bus."

"A bus? What bus?"

"To the County Detention Center in Camp Verde. Court isn't in session this late, so tomorrow morning you'll have your IA."

"Lovely. I've always wanted one. What is an IA?"

"Initial appearance with the judge. By live video."

I was almost, but not quite, speechless. I said, "DNA, retinal scan, arraignment by Skype. From jail! All this for little me? For being in the wrong place at the wrong time?"

He had probably heard plenty of rants like this, sarcastic and angry, but I couldn't stop. I tried to modulate my voice. "I can tell you now, you're wasting your time and your tax-payers' money. I have no 'priors,' have never been arrested and I have no contagious diseases. Do I really look like a threat?"

He looked me over. I knew that at that moment he really saw me for the first time. His silence told me I had raised doubts. He said, "Uh, no Ma'am. It was just a misdemeanor."

Encouraged, I said, "I am not a spy or a terrorist or a threat of any kind. I've only seen that retina thing in spy movies."

"The scan is quick and accurate. It applies to higher levels of security, too. Terrorism taught us to use better technology. But now I think of it...." He opened a desk drawer and pulled out a thin notebook, quickly flipped through the pages, then said. "Right. Your charge doesn't require a retina scan."

I scrubbed the last trace of moisture from my cheeks and hardened my mouth. I was fed up, in spite of my small victory.

He said, "Wait here."

I didn't move. I thought, *I have a choice? He left me alone. He's more sure than I am that I won't go completely berserk or try to run.* I waited in the metal chair with my eyes closed, mind whirling. A sound startled me. The phone in my leather sport bag on the desk. I hesitated before I reached for it. Why did I feel guilty for touching my own belongings? Without looking to see who it was, I turned it off.

The tension in my body began to intrude on the roiling thoughts in my mind. I stood, shrugged my shoulders and flexed my back and knees to relieve the pain. Voices caught my attention. Another blue-uniformed officer entered, his hand on the arm of a young man whose feet dragged, whose face was a stark mask. Embarrassed for him, I looked away just as the two disappeared behind another partition. The mumbled sounds of someone else being booked fed into the ambience of humiliation in the room. I couldn't *not* hear it, but I closed my eyes and tried to think of my grandmother, even of Betty at her peak of competence and assertiveness. What would they do in this situation?

The prompt to myself to calm down and think didn't work. The heat of resentment rose in my gut with the memory of the police officer's hands patting me down, his hostility today and during our first encounter the day of the murder. A thought stabbed me. What if Benson killed Carrie? His behavior might be logical, after all. Surprise and guilt could be behind it.

Deputy Hall returned. I opened my eyes and glanced at the big round clock on the wall. Twenty minutes had ticked off. When Hall sat down, I was surprised to see an actual expression on the man's face. It was a subtle difference from the professional mask he wore earlier. I couldn't define it except to say his face was softer.

"I had a word with the arresting officer," he said. "The charge against you is a misdemeanor. Those don't require a retinal scan or DNA. We usually issue a citation. We're going to O.R. you."

He must have seen my confusion. He said, "Release you on your own recognizance."

"I can go?"

"You have no outstanding warrants and everything else checked out. I'll issue you a citation. You sign the citation to say you'll return for an appointed court date. It's called 'a promise to appear'."

"I can do that. I will." It sank in slowly. "I can leave now?"

He nodded. "No more processing, no jail. No rap session with the judge tomorrow. When you do go to court, the judge could dismiss the case." He hesitated. "If he finds you guilty, you might get a fine. Or community service." Then he smiled. It was the most beautiful smile, showing the whitest, loveliest teeth I have ever seen.

"That sounds...thank you. Thank you so much. So, my dog? I have to go get him."

"He's at the Humane Society on Sundog Ranch Road. It's closed now but I phoned the director at home. He's going to pull the dog, bring him to his house for the night."

"Oh, God. Thank you!"

"The dog will have to go back to the shelter first thing in the morning but not to one of the cages. He'll be up front, in the manager's office. You can pick him up there. They open at seven."

I thanked him again while a new challenge swept into my thoughts. How could I get home? It was too far to walk. I didn't have my credit cards with me or enough cash for a cab. Who could I call?

Chapter Thirteen

Garvin didn't sound a bit surprised to get a call from the Sheriff's booking facility at eight forty-five in the evening. In fact, he sounded excited. He promised he'd be there 'in a flash.' I watched for his car while I stood at the window in the outer foyer. The desk officer, still silent and indifferent, ignored me.

Garvin eased up at the curb up in a long, low-slung black car. I burst out the door, ran to the curb and let myself in. I sat back in the leather seat and took a deep breath, inhaled stale cigarette smoke as gratefully as if it were an ocean breeze. In that awkward moment of realized safety and relief, I leaned forward to pat the dashboard and asked, "What kind of car is this?"

"Two thousand fifteen Trans Am. The bitch is beautiful isn't she?" He grinned at me. There at the curb the lighting was good enough to reveal his five-o-clock shadow, emphasize the keenness of his blue eyes and underscore his masculinity. *Well,* I thought, *if I can notice that, maybe I'm not so traumatized after all.*

Garvin, in turn, made a show of examining my face and arms. I said, "What are you doing?"

"Looking for the bruises."

"What?"

"From the beatings--with the rubber hose."

"Don't be ridic...." I smiled a little.

He pulled the car away, shifting gears smoothly. "You're more interesting than one would think, Allie Davis."

"Because I got arrested? I'd much rather be boring."

"Hell, you might even be hiding a tramp stamp."

"A what?"

"A tattoo. Hearts and flowers, maybe some guy's initials someplace interesting. Like the small of your back or the inside of your thigh."

"Now you're getting a little too personal."

"What was it, then, picking flowers in the park? A little indiscreet use of substance? Surely not drunk and disorderly? You're not the disorderly type."

"Not disorderly enough to do illegal drugs."

"So...?"

"Stop hinting, Garvin. I have no intention of keeping it a secret because I didn't do anything wrong. I got arrested for"--I put the words in air-quotes with two fingers of both hands--"failure to obey a lawful order."

He questioned me with his eyes. I lifted my chin forward at the road he wasn't watching.

He turned his attention, then said, "Okay. I'm taking you to the nearest Starbucks for a 'why bother.' Then you can give me the whole story."

I didn't have the will to object. The coffee shop was almost empty. I hurried to the bathroom. At the sink, I spent more time washing my hands than required for sanitation, then splashed cool water on my face many times before I dried with paper towels. Not that the booking facility had been actually dirty.

In the seating area, I chose a table in the corner with my back to the wall. Garvin came from the counter holding our hot drinks. For some reason, I noticed things I hadn't seen before. His legs, long and lean, were the slightest bit bowed. A subtle swagger accented the click of pointed-toe cowboy boots against the tile floor. He had pulled his long, greying hair into a short knot at the nape of his neck. Crows-feet emphasized his dark blue eyes. A few deep wrinkles bracketed his mouth. He smiled again and from a few feet away I didn't notice the stains on his teeth, just the way his eyes crinkled at the corners and the square angle of his jaw.

He put the cups on the table and pulled out the chair beside me instead of the one directly across. I sipped the 'why bother' he set before me, a decaf latte with skim milk, aptly named.

"Enjoy," he said. He watched me while I sipped, then said, "For a woman who's just been arrested, your hair is much too neat. Looks like you just had it done."

Where did that come from? I wondered. The last thing I expected to hear that evening was a compliment. I said, "I don't get it done. I just get it cut." My hair is dark brown, almost black, with a natural wave that either draws compliments or provokes envy from my friends.

Garvin gulped his coffee, then fiddled with the black band on his wrist, a combination watch and activity tracker I had never seen him without. He noticed. "My Fitbit," he said. "Ten thousand steps today."

I smiled politely.

"I turned off the 'get going' alarm. I don't need it. I'll be damned if I let myself get paunchy and lazy like most men my age. Now, let's hear about your thousand or so steps to jail."

I nodded. I knew for sure that my story was one for the grandchildren. When I finished, Garvin sat back and looked at me with an intensity I didn't understand. Perhaps he meant to summon more details, more information. At any rate, he didn't like my silence. I looked away.

Finally, he said, "What? What problem are you chewing on?"

"Zayd. I can't stop wondering if he's okay. He's such a good dog. He's an athlete, actually."

"A what?"

"He loves to run, so toward the end of a walk I sometimes let him off the leash and tell him 'go home.' He races off and I find him waiting for me at the front door."

"Uh-huh. My ex-wife used to try that with me. It didn't work."

I laughed but it piqued my curiosity. "Your ex-wife? Chris' mother, Betty's niece?"

"The same."

"Did you marry again afterward, like she did?"

"Marriage is what happens when dating goes too far. I've been able to abstain. From marriage, that is."

I sipped my coffee. Garvin was charming tonight, but where was that other side of his personality Betty had warned me about? I said, "Okay. Turn about is fair play. Let's talk about the problems *you're* chewing on."

"None, lady-friend. I faced my inner demons long ago. Now they're my best friends."

"I'm not sure what to make of that."

"Truth is, I've got no demons. I'm fine with me, and if other people aren't fine with me, then I don't give a shit."

"Internal point of reference. Good for you." I put the strap of my purse over my shoulder and shifted in the booth, indicating I was ready to go. He was not.

He asked, "Last Sunday when Lieutenant Grozny questioned you, you told him you didn't see anything, right? So why did you go back today?"

"Just to put it all to rest, really, to let it *go*." I didn't say I now felt *it* would not let *me* go. In case I wasn't clear, I added, "If I say I don't want to get involved in a murder investigation it sounds cold, but there's no reason I should be involved. I'm sorry the poor woman is dead, but I'll let the police do their job. Let *them* figure it out. I have enough to figure out with my clients."

"Woman talk."

"What? It's counseling, not just 'woman talk'. And I do have some men clients."

He said, "When men get together to talk, we talk! Sometimes we even insult each other. When women get together it's like the church choir gets together for an organ recital. And by '*organ,*' I don't mean *music*."

"Women are just a bunch of hypochondriacs? Are you sexist, Garvin?"

He downed the last of his coffee and smiled at me with his mouth closed. That's when I noticed it. Garvin was left-handed. I missed his next few words.

When I recovered, I heard him say,"...figuring them out, Chris tells me you're a good therapist. He needs the counseling. Poor kid..."

"He's a grown man, Garvin, even if he is your son."

"Poor kid is a bubble off plumb."

"A bubble off....?" I did a mental double-take before I understood the metaphor. I said, "That's a strange way to refer to your own son."

"Well, he's a good kid, but.... He likes you and you're helping him. How much has he told you about his childhood?"

The conversation had strayed to a forbidden zone. Client confidentiality was an ethical duty I took seriously. I couldn't discuss Chris with anyone without his permission, not even his father, and Chris had not written his father's name on a release form. I smiled back at Garvin. "A bubble off plumb? So you're a carpenter, or a builder?"

"Among other things. I'm repairing the back steps at Aunt Betty's house. One of my more pleasant duties there."

"Speaking of Betty, please don't say anything to her about this...about my...."

"Your crimes? Your illegal activities? Your brush with the law?"

"You're enjoying this, aren't you, Garvin?"

"Sure. But I'm good at secrets. Excellent, if I do say. So, about Chris...."

"I can't talk about him. Not about any of my clients, or even admit that a particular person *is* a client. Unless they give me permission."

He nodded silently, staring at me. He said, "A lot of secrets there too, behind those big brown eyes."

***

I turned the key to my apartment door, expecting the unexpected, as if it was the first time I had been to this place, as if it was the home of a stranger. I flipped on the ceiling light and closed the door. No stranger greeted me and no familiar welcome from the dog, either. I was alone with myself. I walked aimlessly from room to room until I became focused enough to get ready for bed.

In my pajamas, I thought of the ice cream in the freezer. Binge for the second time in a week? The thought brought more confusion about who I had become. Had my eating disorder appeared again, this many years after I fought it to submission? Stress could take me back to a dysfunctional past if I let it. So went my inner dialogue, until I decided my best reason to reject a relapse was that I had to wake up early and alert, to pick up Zayd.

I turned on the TV and sat on the sofa to relax. With the remote, I flipped through a dozen channels, watching split seconds of assorted stupidity and mayhem. I turned off the TV and got up. The apartment was not designed for pacing--no hallway, not enough floor space to work up a stride.

My unruly thoughts darted back to Zayd. They had kidnapped him, violently. What happened to him at the animal shelter before the shelter's director took him home? What had all that done to him? And what would Kim say when she found out?

Chapter Fourteen

On the way to the animal shelter the next morning, I struggled from lack of sleep. More than the seven hours of sleep missed last night, I needed a long, healing interlude of blessed unconsciousness, one that would last until this waking nightmare turned into a normal dream.

At the shelter, the seemingly normal sound of barking dogs met me. It produced an unexpected chill. When echoing off concrete, the noise of excited animals turned chaotic and deviant. A shudder of pity for the caged animals shook me, then pity for anything or anyone caged.

I gave the receptionist my name and Zayd's name. "I'll call the manager," she said.

Within minutes, the manager walked out and handed me his leash. "He's a nice animal," she said. I didn't glance up or answer her. I had eyes only for the dog. It was rude but I didn't care. I looked into Zayd's eyes, ran my hands over his head, his ears, his neck, his back, all the way to the tip of his tail while the manager watched me. Last, I checked his collar and saw the tags were all there. Satisfied, I straightened up and looked at the woman long enough to thank her. She smiled and returned to her office. The receptionist reached over the counter with release papers in her hand. It took me a few seconds to sign them, then we were out of there.

By eight o'clock, I had him home, fed, petted and pampered. I invited him up on the sofa with me. He sat upright, so like a person I hugged him, hair on my office clothes be damned. I scratched his chin and neck. He lifted his head so I could scratch his chest. Then he sank down, his forelegs so long his paws hung off the edge of the sofa. He looked contented. He looked and acted just like he always did. I hoped he was as unfazed by his recent trauma as he appeared.

I left the apartment at eight-thirty, in time to stop for a second cup of coffee to go, plenty of time to get to the office and meet my nine o'clock client with caffeine-fueled eyes wide open.

I had accepted Betty's office, along with her clients. Like many commercial enterprises in central Prescott, it was originally a modest, two-story residence located on a quiet but easily accessible side street. A renovation years before had created two office suites. I had the downstairs, which included a tiny sitting room used as a waiting room. The larger room was the office and consulting room. A bathroom and tiny kitchen completed the suite. The upstairs housed an architect, who entered via an outside staircase and private door.

I parked my car in the small lot in back and went to the door juggling purse, espresso and briefcase. I started to put the key into the lock. It was scarred and protruding, the wood around it splintered. I stepped back and looked again. The inward-swinging door was ajar by an inch, slightly off the hinges, askew inside the frame.

I put the coffee cup down on the concrete walk, let my purse slide off my arm and placed it and the briefcase beside the cup. A gentle push of one hand sent the office door swinging open. I stepped back and aside. Nothing. I leaned in to look. No intruder in sight. The sitting room was undisturbed but through the open doorway between it and the consulting room, I saw the damage. A hundred white pages and two dozen manila file folders lay on the dark blue carpet of the consulting room.

I stepped inside, leaving the door open behind me. At the threshold to the inner room, I stopped and took off my shoes. I skated, toes first, through the scattered debris. In the corner, I saw what I dreaded. The locked metal file cabinet had been pried open. Its contents were what lay on the floor, pages of sensitive, personal, confidential client information. I stood for a moment in disbelief then, thought, *'previously* confidential information.' I looked around but saw no other damage. Red lights on both my desk phone and the answering machine were blinking.

"Hello?"

I started, whirled around. *What now?*

Amy Aren stood on the threshold of the outer door, one trembling hand pressed over her lips. Her other hand white-knuckled the handle of the baby carrier. I thought, *What lousy timing for a drop-in! I have to send her away.*

I looked again and really saw. The baby held a blue plastic rattle in one tiny fist. His eyes were clear, wide and curious as he looked around. His mother's eyes blurred with tears. Her usually pale face appeared red and swollen. The baby was fine. Amy was not. Every nuance spoke of extreme emotional distress. She was a young mother in crisis. I couldn't send her away. I motioned her in. She stepped into the waiting room but stopped at the threshold of the consulting room and blinked at the littered floor.

I stood straight and summoned my counselor persona. "Amy, I'm sorry for the mess. I just discovered it myself. Wait a minute, please."

She watched while I gathered enough papers to clear a path to the sofa so she could sit down. Then I put my shoes on and went to close the outer door. I hoped it would close all the way, so the lock could engage. It didn't. My throat tightened. The landlord would have to replace the whole door, with a new lock. I'd have to call him, then he would call his insurance company *and* the police. *Damn!*

I went back in to say, "Give me just a few more minutes, then we'll talk." I went out and grabbed my purse and briefcase from the sidewalk. The coffee with cream and a shot of espresso was growing cool and scummy. I came in, closed the interior door for privacy and put my things down on the desk.

Amy had placed the baby's carrier beside her on the sofa but she didn't touch him or look at him. I murmured, "Excuse me just another minute, please" and turned my back to her. I called the client scheduled to arrive in fifteen minutes and caught him just before he left, in time to cancel. I told him only that I had an emergency.

Finally, I turned back to Amy. She said, "Allie I'm sorry for barging in like this."

"What happened?"

She looked away, reached out to her son. He grasped the forefinger of her trembling hand in his baby fist. "I came because there's something you need to know. Last night I asked Chris to move out."

I was already too unsettled to be shocked. "Tell me about it."

She pulled a tissue from the diaper bag. "I told you Chris doesn't like to hold the baby. Well, yesterday afternoon I had a doctor's appointment. I told Chris it was time he started to act like a real dad, like he did with Hailee. I left Buddy with him." She paused. "I...I don't know if Chris told you, but the psychiatrist he went to put him on a load of medications."

The issue of Chris's medications was important, but I wondered why it was relevant to her story. I asked, "Do you know what they are? The names?"

"I don't remember all the names, but I know what kind they are. One is an antidepressant. One is what he called an anxiolytic--for anxiety. There's a third one he said was for anxiety, too, but I looked it up on-line and it said 'antipsychotic'."

She stopped to wipe a bit of drool from the baby's pink chin, then looked up to meet my eyes. "When I came home, I knew Chris must have taken too much because he was holding the baby, but just barely. He looked all weak and limp like he was drunk, but it wasn't alcohol."

"Are you sure?"

"I could tell he hadn't been drinking. It was the meds. He could barely talk. Buddy was fretting and about to fall off his lap. When I picked the baby up he was wet and hungry. Chris hadn't fed him the whole bottle of formula."

"You must have been very upset."

She drew a deep breath. "I can't trust him with the baby, Allie. I...I even started to think about Hailee again. Hailee and Carrie...Hailee and Chris. Oh, God! I started to wonder--what if it wasn't a crib death?" She lowered her head and shook it from side to side. Her long blond hair draped down, hiding her face.

I knew I couldn't let my mind go where her fears had led her. I had to focus. I asked, "What did Chris say? What happened?"

"I asked him to move out."

"Did he?"

"He's   gone."

Chapter Fifteen

After Amy left the office, I picked up the rest of the client files. I made no attempt to organize them, just stacked them into two jumbled piles on top of the file cabinet. The paper and file folder corners stuck out at every angle, which made the stacks more circular than oblong.

At my desk, I pushed around the stapler, tape dispenser, Post-it notes and other implements on the desk-top, rearranging them, trying to summon calm and organization. The red, incoming call light on the phone blinked again. I ignored it. Before I left the evening before, I had silenced the ring and forwarded calls to the answering machine.

Soon I was composed enough to talk. I made a series of calls to deal with the break-in. First, the owner/landlord of the office to report the damage, then my other appointments for the day to cancel. Last, I called my professional organization's attorney to ask what I should do about the twenty serious breaches of client confidentiality the crime represented.

When I put the phone down other questions came. *Why? Why would anyone want what was in these files enough to break in? Had the vandal targeted just one or all of my clients? Was it a senseless act of destruction or perhaps the leading edge of some new fraud that targeted multiple people with mental health issues?* The thought of a perpetrator finding a way to heap trauma and pain on already-vulnerable souls chilled me. I stood and began to pace.

"What's this?"

It was a man's voice. I turned. Lieutenant Grozny. Law enforcement again. I had hung up with the building's owner just a few minutes before. The police couldn't have gotten here that fast.

The Lieutenant stood in the outer doorway, head cocked in obvious interest at signs of criminal damage, then he swaggered into the consulting room. His alert gaze took in the damaged file cabinet and the heap of disordered papers. "What happened here?"

I folded arms across my mid-section and faced him. This would be another interrogation like the one at the crime scene on Sunday. Then I realized my feet were still bare. I had taken off my earrings and the silk scarf around my neck. I felt naked under his stare. I said, "What are you doing here? You have no right to barge into my office."

"The door was open. I didn't barge. I entered legally, Miss Davis."

"It's 'Ms. Davis.' And this is a private office. No one called you."

"Why didn't you report it?"

"I called the owner. He's reporting it."

"I'm as unhappy to be here as you are, Miss Davis, but what an interesting coincidence. This morning I went through arrest records from yesterday. Officer Benson wrote a good report. You were back at the murder scene again."

"It was nothing. I didn't...."

"We're going to talk about why you showed up there a second time." He gestured at the damage in the office. "I'll want you to explain this, too."

He walked over and sat down in my high-backed leather desk chair. He tilted his head and said slowly, "Let's do this again. Did you know the victim we found on Sunday?"

I didn't answer. What nerve he had to sit in my chair, the therapist's chair. If he expected me to sit on the clients' sofa, he was dead wrong. I stood straighter and held my elbows until they hurt. "I told you I didn't know her."

"Then tell me again."

I said, "You need to leave."

"Either you answer my questions here or we can go back to the station. If you didn't know the decedent, do you know anyone who did know her?"

He had me trapped. I said, "I'm acquainted with Garvin Kastner and Chris Aren. And Amy Aren."

He nodded. "I saw you talking to Kastner the day of the murder. And Chris Aren."

He already knew. He had been testing me.

"How often do you walk in the woods?"

"Never. Well, I hike sometimes, but those woods-- never before."

He asked, "Who else do you know who might have known the victim?"

"Betty Jackson. This is her office. I've been filling in for her. She's not well."

"Is Chris Aren your client? Or Kastner?"

"I won't answer that. Questions are off limits about whether someone is or isn't my client. Confidentiality. It's a Federal law. HIPPA."

"Well, aren't you the aces for confidentiality?" He shot a glance toward the invaded file cabinet.

"I will handle it. I will send each and every client a 'Breach of Confidentiality' notice. I will do anything else the attorney advises me to do."

He edged forward an inch on the chair so his feet planted wider and harder on the floor. He leaned toward me. I heard the squeak of leather on leather, and smelled the earthy scents of man and his gear.

"I know about the law, Miss Davis--penalties for breaking the law. They apply to all of us equally. If you withhold evidence pertinent to a murder investigation, you are a criminal."

The look on his face would wilt daises. I coached myself not to be intimidated. Behind him, the light on the desk phone began to blink again. With Grozny glaring at me, the light felt as jarring as an insistent ring.

I said, "I'm not withholding anything. I don't know anything! I don't *want* to know anything about the poor woman *or* who murdered her."

He turned off his sour face and stood. He said, "I will coordinate and share information with the officer who investigates this break-in. You will remain in this area, available for questioning, until further notice. You will keep your court date for the charge against you from yesterday. If you fail to do either, you will be arrested and jailed." He turned to go. Over his shoulder, he said, "I promise you that."

I wanted to throw the telephone at his retreating back. Instead, I went to answer it. The light stopped blinking before I could pick it up. There would be messages on the machine.

Phones and messages. My intent to check the machine short-circuited with another thought. The night before in the booking facility, I had turned off my personal phone and hadn't turned it on again. I bent to the bottom drawer of the desk, where I had stashed my purse.

"Prescott police!"

I jerked upright. Another uniformed officer and the building's owner, Larry Childreth, walked in without an invitation. I stood to face them while my head swam. Suddenly I was terribly thirsty and a fog of unreality threatened to descend. I told myself *no, no time for it. I have to deal with this.*

It didn't take long to report how I found the break-in. Both men were polite, efficient and matter of fact, considering they had encountered a barefoot, disheveled, distracted woman who stood in a ruined office. Childreth reassured me he would replace the door within an hour but the file cabinet was my responsibility. Another chore added to the growing list in my head. I would have to buy a new file cabinet today.

The minute they left, I retrieved my phone, turned it on and listened to four voice mails from Kim. The first was "Allie, are you okay? Why don't you pick up?" The second was, "Why were you arrested?" The last, in a chilled tone I had never heard from my friend, "Where is he, Allie? Where is my dog?"

Chapter Sixteen

She answered my call on the first ring. I blurted, "Kim, Zayd is safe. He's okay. He's at my apartment right now."

"He's okay?" I heard the doubt in her voice.

"He seems fine. Like always." She didn't respond. "I guess I could take him to a vet and have him checked if you want me to."

"What happened, Allie? Why were you arrested?"

"Wait a second. How did you know I was in jail? Well, actually it was a booking facility."

"A sheriff's deputy, Hill, he said his name was, called me last night. He told me you had Zayd with you when they arrested you. He asked if you stole him."

"Another crime they wanted to lay on me! He had on his tags, Kim. That's how they got your telephone number. Would I have left his tags on if I stole him?"

"I guess they thought you might be that dumb."

"They took him, Kim. There was nothing I could do until this morning. I am so sorry."

"Hill asked about the search and rescue team in Yuma County. He checked to see if you told them the truth."

"I never dreamed they would call you."

"They respect search and rescue dogs. Anyway, then he asked if I knew any law enforcement back home. EMTs always do. I told him I'm engaged to Lon Raney, which made it better, somehow."

"What, every deputy sheriff in Arizona knows every other? They're all brothers?"

"Seems that way. So, Zayd was stuck at the animal shelter all night? Those places are...."

"No, no! The director of the shelter took him home for the night. In the morning, he brought him back and left him in an office there. That's where I picked him up."

"Tell me more about it Saturday. I'll be there in the morning. Can you and Zayd stay safe and out of jail until then?"

Still smiling, I put the phone down, lowered my forehead to the desk, closed my eyes and rested. Kim wasn't furious at me. She didn't blame me.

After a few minutes, I sat up and went to sort out the client files. My hand hesitated over the manila folder on top. It was Chris Aren's file. A strange coincidence, since I had just seen his wife. Then it struck me--the file was on top because it was in the center and on the very bottom of the scattered mess on the floor, the last one I picked up. There were two others before it in the alphabetically arranged file drawer, but it was the first one tossed down by the intruder. I rifled through the pile to find Chris's psychosocial assessment and therapy session notes. They were near the top, also. I went back to the desk and double checked the dates in my appointment book to be sure I had them all, then arranged the file in date order.

Numbed by a slurry of questions without answers, I placed the file on my desk and sat down, staring at it. What finally registered was the pages didn't lie flat. I pulled out a sheet. Small creases marred its left edge. I selected several other pages. I made out faint indentations along the left sides. The image came, of someone holding them tightly in the fingers of their left hand. I'm right handed. Was Chris was the intruder's target? If so, was it Chris himself, or someone else who wanted to know--what?

It was beyond comprehension. I stood up abruptly and turned toward the door. I wanted to get out of there but no way would I leave the office until a new door hung on strong hinges and I had a key in my hand. I went to get a glass of water, reminding myself, from my crisis worker days, that tears and stress cause dehydration.

Reconstructing the rest of the files was tedious work. I was almost finished when the landlord and his helper arrived with the new door. They got it up on the hinges and secured in minutes. The landlord eyed me as he came into the office. He placed the key in my hand, raised one eyebrow and said, "I leased this place to Betty Jackson. I don't normally let people sub-lease. Her reputation and my good nature are the only things caused me to let you in here."

"Betty and I are very grateful, Mr. Childreth. And the clients are happy they didn't have to change offices."

"I'm thinking this mess was some dumb-ass kids' idea of fun but if it happens again, you're out."

"I understand." When I was alone in my newly locked office, I shook my head like a dog shaking off water. I had to shrug off, for the second time today, a threat from an irate man.

At last the client notes were in their folders, the folders in alphabetical order stacked in three neat piles on my desk. I sat down, leaned back and pushed the hair from my face with both hands. As far as I could tell, not one psychosocial assessment or therapy note was missing from any of the files. Even a few small sticky-notes with scribbled reminders to myself were there. Then what was the point? Random vandalism, as the landlord suggested? Or another mystery, something to do with Chris?

My work wasn't over for the day. I tried my new key in the office door, wary of taking one small chance at continuing a contrary chain of events. I needed to hurry to the mall to buy a new file cabinet. At the last minute, I decided to shop on-line. It was a good decision. I followed the successful search with a phoned-in order. I used my most persuasive voice to earn a promise for next-day delivery of the expensive piece of office furniture.

I found the attorney for my professional organization had faxed me an official breach of confidentiality notification form. I made twenty copies, one for each of the current clients, grateful that Betty had taken home files of former clients to store there.

By the time I had filled out the first form, my growling stomach complained about no breakfast or lunch and my droopy eyelids complained about a lack of caffeine, since I had thrown out the morning's tepid coffee. I closed my eyes to think it through. Hungry or not, how could I leave the office? The outer door hadn't provided enough security. The door between the reception area and consulting room didn't have a lock. Damage to the file cabinet prevented me from locking up the files. Hunger provided strong enough motivation to solve the issue. I reasoned that the break-in happened last night and was unlikely to happen again today in broad daylight. I rummaged through the top desk drawer until I found a key, then crammed all the files into two bottom drawers and locked them. I paused long enough to call a local security company and inquire about an alarm system before I went out to a very late lunch.

Fast food had never before given me heartburn. Maybe it was because I kept thinking of the break-in, then Amy and Chris, the tragedy of their baby girl's death, and their infant boy who now lacked a competent, care-giving father. It wouldn't leave me alone.

At my desk again, I called Chris's cell phone. "Hi, Chris. How are you?"

"Okay."

"Amy told me what happened. I don't think you should wait until next week to see me. Why don't you come in today?"

Chapter Seventeen

Blond stubble shadowed Chris's usually clean-shaven face. His clothing appeared rumpled but clean. The good news was that he was clear-eyed and self-possessed, not sedated as Amy had last seen him. I bolstered myself to deliver a stern, Dutch-uncle-talk session that some counselors jokingly call *slap therapy*. Not long after the first hellos, I said, "I need you to really talk to me now, Chris. Tell me what's going on."

"Yeah."

"It's the only way we're going to get anywhere, to make things better."

He pushed his back harder against the sofa. "Did you know Amy told me to move out?"

"Yes, of course. I spoke to her. Why, Chris?"

"She left Buddy with me yesterday. She said when she came home I was--she said *comatose*."

"She told me."

"She said I was almost comatose with him in my arms. She was crying and she was pissed. She was beyond pissed. It was a scene."

"I'm sorry."

"I've never seen her like that."

"Where are you staying now?"

"With a friend from Embry-Riddle."

"Okay, so you're with a friend for now, and Amy and the baby are okay. Let's talk about you. You told me *when* your problems started, but never really told me *how* and *why* they started."

He sighed and rubbed his hand across his face before he answered. "When she brought the baby home--I think that was when the panic and the depression set in. What was depression? It was new to me. I didn't know why I stopped wanting to get out of bed in the morning or why my performance at work was just automatic, like my heart wasn't in it."

"Yes, those are symptoms of depression."

"My sex drive went to shit, too. I guess that was okay by Amy, her being post-partum and so busy with Buddy."

"That's not unusual. Men can have reduced sexual interest, even performance problems. On the other hand, problems can be a side effect of some antidepressants. Tell me what you're on."

"I don't remember them all."

"Maybe you need to talk to your psychiatrist about them."

He didn't response. I asked, "Will you bring them or a list of them when you come for your scheduled appointment next week?"

"Sure."

"Chris, you took a lot of medications when you were supposed to be taking care of Buddy."

I saw the muscles around his mouth tighten. He leaned his head far back. His eyes gazed at the ceiling. He said nothing for a second, then turned an angry face toward me.

He said, "The police came to interview me about Carrie Lougee. It was her last week--the one killed in the woods."

I nodded.

"They acted like I could know what happened, or why. We knew her, sure, but she hasn't been to sit for Buddy at all. First my Hailee, then Carrie. Enough, damn it, enough!"

I saw his fists clench at his sides. I had no comforting response to offer. I waited. He was distraught, yes, but he had side-stepped my line of inquiry. I had to ask. "Chris, has alcohol ever been a problem for you? Recreational drugs, maybe marijuana? Meth, heroin?"

He leaned forward, fists pushing down against his thighs and snorted in such indignation droplets of mucous fell from his nose. In a tight voice, he said, "I have never abused alcohol or illegal drugs. I was an athlete, and a good one."

"I know."

"I am an adult, a married man, a father. I am a teacher at a prestigious college, an investigator of air craft crashes. You think I'm a pot-head, a Fentanyl freak or a heroin addict?"

"Chris, that's not what I said. Not what I implied. Please, let's back up. Can you understand that I have to ask questions that may seem like an insult, even when I doubt they apply to you? I have to ask if you don't volunteer information."

His face remained set, his blue eyes intense. I said nothing but returned his stare. He collapsed back against the sofa and as his anger subsided, he appeared exhausted. In our mutual silence, my unspoken question persisted: *why was Chris so anxious when he watched the baby that he had to medicate himself to the point of somnolence?* Intuition suggested the answer.

I said, "Chris I know this counseling has been hard for you but you've been committed to it, committed to get back to normal. It's not easy to talk about your feelings. A written questionnaire might be easier to deal with."

"*Easy* isn't necessarily my style."

"I get that. So, there is a screening tool I'd like to share with you."

"I already did that Beck thing for depression."

"Yes, you did. This is a questionnaire that applies to people with Obsessive Compulsive Disorder. It may not apply to you, but we need to see."

His shrug contradicted the trace of interest I saw in his face. I said, "I'd like to read the introduction aloud before you do it. The intro defines the words *obsessions* and *compulsions*."

"Okay."

I went to the bottom drawer of the broken file cabinet, pulled the folder on OCD and placed it on a clipboard. I went back, sat down and began to read.

"It says, '*Obsessions are thoughts, impulses or mental images that intrude on your thinking often. The thoughts, impulses or images can be upsetting, things that actually disgust you, or senseless things that you would never do. For example, a reoccurring thought or impulse to harm your children in some way*'."

Before going on to the 'compulsions' section, I glanced up quickly to see his reaction. A pale mask of horror looked back at me. Chris launched himself from the sofa. I started, stood up. The clipboard slid off my lap with a thunk. He fled, slamming both doors behind him before I could move or speak.

Chapter Eighteen

My client, Chris Aren, had just bolted out of the office. I remained standing. I had seen that kind of reaction only once before during many years of counseling. I was confounded. Should I go after him? Wait an hour and then at least call him? My better judgement told me to leave him alone. It took me only a few minutes to forward the office phone to my cell phone. If he wanted to talk to me, he could.

Mental and emotional exhaustion caught up with me. I put things away, locked up and went home. What else could I do after the last two incredible days?

At home, I fed Zayd and took him for a walk. He frisked, with too much energy. I, on the other hand, tottered after him like a zombie, too tired to think. It's all I remember before I went home and fell into bed, into a long, restless sleep.

***

The questions didn't go away. They woke me the next morning before I could orient myself. The thought, *Why did Chris run?* eclipsed all else. When self-awareness came, I realized I felt rested enough to think things through, to understand what was previously inexplicable. The most urgent question demanded, *Why did Chris feel such horror when I read him the example of obsessing about harm to one's child? Because in fact he did have those obsessive thoughts? Or because he had already acted on them?* Motionless in bed, I ruminated. Either explanation for his behavior was horrifying. *Maybe if I lie here long enough I can solve it,* I thought.

Zayd knew I was awake. His nose poked at the bed covers, his tail wagged persuasively, his brown eyes wide and smiling. I got up. This was Friday. I had only two clients today, but I needed to get to the office to accept delivery of the new file cabinet.

The normality of my morning routine with Zayd felt reassuring. After our run and my usual preparations, on a sudden impulse, I put him in the car for the drive to the office. I left him while I went to the door alone, wary of another break-in. The new door was intact, everything inside undisturbed. It looked fine.

Back outside, I discovered when Zayd was in my parked car, I didn't have to lock it. If someone came too close, he stood up and silently bared his teeth. It was enough to deter the most foolhardy individual.

In the office, he made himself at home, lying down beside the clients' sofa. The delivery man arrived minutes later. Before he wheeled in my new, solid oak file cabinet, I gave Zayd the *stay* command so he watched the process calmly, without moving. I gave the delivery man a twenty dollar bill, enough to convince him to take away the damaged metal cabinet. Then I tried the key in the new cabinet lock. Secure. Instead of dropping the key in the top desk drawer, I decided to carry it in my purse.

At that point, it occurred to me I owed Betty an explanation of what had happened. She still cared about the clients who not long ago were hers. I would go see her after work. Maybe she could even shed some light on who would have reason and nerve enough to break in and go through their records.

I started to take Zayd back to the apartment but hesitated. I wanted him at the office with me. I called both my afternoon clients and asked if they were allergic to dogs or afraid of dogs. They weren't.

I completed the letters that notified clients about the break-in and took them to the post office. They had to go by certified mail with return receipt.

Everything by the book. Rather, everything on advice from the attorney. I hated this.

Zayd was perfect in the car. He sat up in the back seat and enjoyed the ride. Back at the office, he seemed equally comfortable. Perhaps bored, but comfortable.

My one p.m. client was a young college student I had seen only twice before. The first thing she saw when she entered the office was the dog. He rose to greet her. "Hey, baby!" she said to him. "You are straight hot!" She turned to me. "What's his name?"

"Zayd."

"Zed?"

"No, Zayd."

"What kind of name is that?"

"Oh. Well, the story goes that the owner's brother was studying Arabic while he got ready to deploy to Iraq. The owner had just adopted the dog from a shelter. Her brother thought it would be good luck to name the dog *abundance, prosperity* in Arabic. It's supposed to be pronounced '*Zay-ed*.' Now he's just '*Zayd*.'"

It was an easy session, my client charmed and distracted by the dog. He was both a benefit to me and a detriment to the client's therapeutic process. I decided to tell the young woman and my next client, as well, about the break-in and possible breach of their confidential information, in addition to sending the letters. Both took it very well. I was so happy when both scheduled return appointments. Maybe they wouldn't all desert me.

Later, on the way to Betty's house, I made a concerted effort to forget about the break-in. Instead, I pondered the changes in a person's brain wrought by Alzheimer's. I had read, and still have in my book case, two exceptional books which delve into the mystery of dementia, *Still Alice* and *On Pluto--Inside the Mind of Alzheimer's*. A cautionary thought intruded. Betty's cat, Mange. Would he attack Zayd? I called her.

She said, "A more appropriate question is whether the dog will attack the cat."

"He knows better. He controls his instinctual drives better than some people I know." That seemed to satisfy her.

When she opened her door she greeted me, "Hello, Sweetie, come...." Then she spotted Zayd. Her mouth formed a perfect 'O', her arms went up in surprise then she grabbed the scruff of his neck and planted a kiss on his muzzle. "You gorgeous thing!" she said.

Zayd seldom wagged his tail but he did then. In fact, he looked rather smug, while I was shocked. "Betty! I hope you don't greet every dog that way."

"Course not. If he tolerates cats, I know he's safe. Come in, both of you. I have some lemonade in the ice box."

She must have seen me blink. Her expression changed, fell flat and vacant, but she said nothing. Her unspoken words hung in the air. I tried to imagine her defensive reaction, her thoughts: *"I called it an ice box. So what? That's what my mother used to call it."*

I said, "I never argue with fresh lemonade, Betty."

"Good. Lots of vitamin C." At that second, Mange materialized silently, like a white ghost, from under the sofa. Zayd stiffened but didn't move. The cat spotted him, arched his back, shimmied sideways on his toe pads and hissed. Zayd didn't respond. The cat continued his performance for a few seconds, then broke and darted into the bedroom. Betty and I laughed. I removed Zayd's leash. On the way to the kitchen, Betty's fingertips teased the fur on his back while he attempted to walk three across, as if we were a troika. Only when we went through the narrow doorway did he deign to lag behind us and follow.

I sat down at the table, brushed away a few crumbs of toast, and asked, "How have you been lately, Betty?"

"You mean, how many of my brain cells have died since we last talked? Ask the doctors, Sweetie. I have no idea."

Still Betty, I thought. What else would she say if she dared? I have spent so many working years as a therapist trying to get inside peoples heads, I imagined the thoughts in hers: *"Why, years ago, people who thought and behaved differently were called 'mental.' Now we say they have a mental illness. Alzheimer's dementia isn't one of them. It's an organic disease, a different kind of distress. Kind and truthful can co-exist, can't they?"*

I tried to ease back to safer territory. I said, "If you think Zayd is beautiful, wait until you see his owner. Kim is tall and beautiful, like the Hollywood version of an Apache woman."

"Nothing wrong with that."

"She doesn't act like any stereotype I know. She's coming tomorrow to get Zayd. I'd like you to meet her."

"Of course," Betty said. "I can't wait to see her in person." She went to the refrigerator for a pitcher and poured two glasses of freshly squeezed lemonade. Then she stood on tiptoe to reach into an upper cabinet. I wondered why, but didn't question. She took down a lovely crystal bowl, filled it with water and put it on the floor in front of Zayd before she sat down.

I didn't want to delay the purpose of my visit, unpleasant news. I said, "Betty, I'm sorry to tell you this, but someone broke into the office the other night."

"The office? *My* office? Why in the world....?"

"Nothing was taken. They--whoever it was--didn't damage anything except the file cabinet. I replaced it with a nicer one, solid oak." The look on her face told me Betty didn't care about a new piece of office furniture.

"If nothing was taken, why?"

"I don't know. The files were scattered all over the floor."

"Sounds like a real pig's breakfast."

"I've never seen one of those, but that could describe it. Like someone was looking for something, maybe information about a client or clients."

"I can't imagine...."

"There might be something about one of the clients that someone wanted to know *badly*. It's the only thing that makes sense to me. Some hot marital issue, a child custody issue, or maybe a sexual secret that one person could use against another?"

She shook her head. "I don't think any of my clients--your clients--had those issues or were that intense...that disturbed. Not that I knew of, anyway. Maybe it had to do with money?"

"Money? None of our clients are really wealthy, are they?"

She said, "Seems it's always about money in the end. These damned, greedy, rich people act like they aren't. They use their pretend poverty to be stingy and cheap."

The conversation's ninety-degree turn surprised me. I said, "Let's not worry about it, Betty. Maybe I shouldn't have bothered you but I felt you had a right to know."

"All kinds of mischief going on in the world, Allie. People with blood on their hands."

It was a strange comment. We sat for some time without speaking. Prolonged silences punctuated our conversations more of late. I wondered whether Betty's quiescence served as a deliberate refuge or was a sign of her organic impairment. I knew not to mention my arrest two days before, or yesterday's counseling fiasco with Chris. A person could only cope with so much input at one time.

She finished her lemonade and reached up to tuck her hair behind her ears. Her palms were narrow, fingers long and tapered, an artist's hands. I envied them. Mine were short and thick, a worker's hands. Today she wore a green-striped, knee-length cotton dress with a square neck and three-quarter-length sleeves. She looked as well put together as ever. How ironically appearance could mock reality.

She said, "I wish I could help you figure it out but when facts don't lead me out of a maze, I try intuition."

"Sometimes my intuition leads me out of a maze and right into a fire."

She smiled at the mixed metaphor. "Ah, yes. In Cottonwood." Betty had no problem with remote memories. She continued, "Your intuition made you drive out to the boonies in the middle of the night, didn't it?"

"I knew one or more of my clients were in trouble."

"You saved two lives that night. You kept Kim from killing the child molester. If she had, her life would have ended, too."

"You could look at it that way. But in Yuma, I worked with a man every day, every week for more than a year and didn't know when he killed my best friend."

"Enough. Your self-doubts are a whip for your own back. You didn't know he was a killer because you weren't tuned into him as a client. You can't keep that level of openness and sensitivity to everyone--all their inner conflicts and machinations--you'd go crazy." She hesitated. "Don't criticize me for using that word. I call things by their right names."

"Right names.... Yes. I knew a psychologist who described her clients' issues, all the emotions, the conflicts, all the angst they shared in detail with her during sessions--she called it *'just data.'*"

"Just data? That's ridiculous. If what clients say is just a set of unimportant facts, why does the federal government create such strict laws to keep it secret? Damn near sacred, the way we protect it."

"It's peoples' lives. Sometimes it weighs on me."

She said, "You're the best psychotherapist I know."

"I've made some serious mistakes."

She gave me a look. "Haven't we all?"

I said, "Like when I counseled a very young Mexican man. I wanted to show warmth, show my regard for him. I called him *Meja. Meja* instead of *Mejo.* I called him a little girl."

"Big deal. You think an 'a' instead of an 'o' would make the man question his sexual identity?"

"No, but...."

She smiled. "Maybe decide to go transgender, become a mom to his kids instead of dad?"

I laughed. "No, but I called him a little girl--a sissy."

"It didn't change the way he thought of himself, Allie. It made him think his counselor was a well-meaning gringa who needed Spanish lessons."

Chapter Nineteen

Kim's red Jeep Cherokee pulled up outside my apartment door the next morning and pleasant excitement filled me. Zayd, on the other hand, had been keyed-up for an hour. Some would say he was only responding to my anticipation, but I think he sensed her imminent arrival.

I opened the door. He ran out to meet her, dancing, chuffing, and licking her face. She looked so happy while she smiled and talked to him. A yellow band held back her long black hair. She wore a t-shirt, shorts and Nikes. Her knee was still covered with an ace bandage and beneath it, more bandages. The dog sniffed them briefly, then appeared to dismiss this new feature of his owner's body.

I waited until she and the dog had their reunion, then I hugged her and kissed her on her cheek. I realized my feelings for her verged on the maternal. I don't have a daughter but I adore my son so much it never before occurred to me to regret the lack of a female offspring.

I said, "I'm so glad to see you. How is the knee?"

"It's a bit painful if I turn it the wrong way, but not as much as before the surgery. I'm good."

"Yes, you are. Well, come into the kitchen. I'll make coffee and we can catch up."

"Allie, I've been in the car for an hour, and it's such a beautiful day...."

"Of course."

At High Meadows, Kim let Zayd off the leash. They must have had an unspoken pact not to let each other out of sight, because he didn't stray far to explore.

She and I sat on a bench and talked about nothing but the minutiae of life until we strolled and I gravitated again to the basket swing. We took turns. At first we behaved properly, as grown women should. Then we made the swing turn and spin wildly while we laughed at each other.

After a while, we strolled to the vegetable garden where Kim admired my sprouts of lettuce and the feathery tops of baby carrots. She helped me plant herbs while we talked and joked. We enjoyed the feel of soil in our hands and the fragrances of basil and mint and rosemary. We lingered there for a while, I don't know how long. I lost track of time. On days like that in May, nurturing rays of sun warm the skin and cool mountain breeze ruffle the hair. The earth is brushed with pastel colors and the world turns more slowly on its axis.

Later that afternoon, when I took Kim to the house to meet Betty, Betty was tired and not inclined to conversation. We soon readied ourselves to leave. As fate would have it, Garvin met us coming to the door. "Well, who is this?" he asked, eyeing Kim up and down with undisguised relish. I knew the bandage on her left knee didn't detract from the elegant length and sculpted curves of her legs.

I introduced them while Kim looked back at Garvin, his neat frame, blue eyes and grey-at-the-temples hair pulled back tightly off his tan, even-featured face.

He held their hand-shake a few seconds too long. He asked her, "Do you live here, or just visiting?"

"Passing through, you could say."

"Too bad. Prescott is worth seeing."

It might have been rude, but I interrupted. "See you later, Garvin. Bye, Betty." I linked my arm through Kim's elbow and drew her down the steps, onto the brick walk-way and to my car. We settled in and I pulled the car away from the curb. I asked, "You were attracted to him, weren't you?" Even as I said it, I recalled Betty had asked me the same question.

"Sure. He's an attractive guy."

"Except for the cigarette smell and yellow teeth."

"I get the impression you don't like him."

"I don't know him very well. Anyway, he's right. Prescott isn't just beautiful, it's Old West history preserved. Cowboys and Indians *in vivo*. Why don't you stay a day or two?"

"You know, I could. My suitcases are in the Jeep. I planned to head straight back home but medical leave from work gives me three more days."

"Wonderful."

I loved Kim's company but I had an ulterior motive--I needed my friend's help to sort out the past week's mix of tragedy, absurdity and nebulous circumstances that had me baffled. That evening, we rejected my usual routine of reading or watching TV in favor of lounging on the sofa to sip red wine. The wine, my friend's company and the reassuring presence of the dog relaxed me. I could wait to process my dilemma. I recalled my telephone conversation with her a few days ago. I said, "I'd ask about your father if you wanted to talk about him."

Her face twisted in pain. "He's old and sick, Allie. Not even seventy, but he's had a hard-working life, and it's taking its toll."

"I understand." When Kim turned to look straight into my face, I wondered if I did understand.

She said, "It's not just the diabetes. He has COPD from years of smoking, and half a dozen other medical problems. I'm beginning to see why he wants to quit dialysis."

Silence was my only response.

She continued, "At first I was against it. Of course, I wanted him to stay in treatment. The doctor and the nurses told him he would die if he stopped. Even Mom wanted him to continue. Then yesterday--it was a dialysis day--he asked me to come and sit with him."

"Sounds nice."

"Yeah, *no big deal*." She hesitated.

"Okay. And?"

"I found the dialysis place but somehow I went in the wrong door, a side door that opened right into the treatment room." She drew in her breath and closed her eyes. "All I saw was blood, Allie, the whole room was red with it. It was a bloody room filled with tubes and more tubes of blood that flowed with strange sucking sounds. Like a torture chamber but the people just sat there in those recliner chairs, napping or watching TV. No screams of pain, but it was torture they were going through. It made me sick."

"Oh, Kim."

"All those people hooked up to machines and my dad was one of them. I had to see his blood, too. My stomach turned inside out."

I suppressed a choice curse word before I said, simply, "I'm sorry."

"The nurse ran over and took me out to the reception area. She was really nice about it. She tried to make it sound so normal, like that ugly thing in his chest is a *port* instead of some kind of parasite imbedded in his body."

Unable to say a word, I leaned to her, put my arms around her shoulders and touched my forehead to hers. When I released her, she opened her eyes and said, "I went back in and managed to sit with him and talk to him. All the time, the word *'purgatory'* ran through my mind. Me and my dad in purgatory, marooned, stranded on an island between the land of the living and the land of the dead."

"It's not fair, is it? Life isn't fair."

"He has to do it three days a week, hours at a time. I can't blame Mom for wanting him to keep it up, but asking someone to get tortured on a regular basis is taking your love for them too far.

"It isn't painful, is it?"

"No. But...."

I had to say, "You know, dialysis saves peoples' lives. Millions of people."

"It's different if they're younger. They might be in really good health, other than kidney disease. They might be waiting for a transplant. What isn't fair is for mom and me to ask him to live that way if he doesn't want to. I just don't know what to think or what to say to him about it any more."

"I know you, Kim. All you need to think about is how much you love him. Then you'll say and do what's right, what's in your heart."

She didn't speak for a long time. When she did it was to change the subject. "You know, that telephone conversation we had last week? About when Zayd ran away from you in the woods? The only time he disobeyed my *come* command--since he was a pup, anyway--was the night he chased a man who tried to kill us."

"Whoa." I wondered what were the implications of *that*?

Kim said, "After we talked on the phone, I was confused about what was going on in Prescott with you and Zayd while I was stuck in Camp Verde. Then I felt guilty for thinking about anything at all except Dad.

Chapter Twenty

On Sunday morning, Kim and I both woke early. I went to get the newspapers while she took Zayd out for a quick run. When I returned, Zayd had settled down in the living room by the sofa where his two-person pack leader had slept. She was in the kitchen making coffee.

I divided the newspaper into sections to easily share and peruse, then placed it on the coffee table. By then, Kim was on the phone, talking to her parents. When she put the phone away, I went to the kitchen to join her. She looked so happy and relaxed, I could tell they had told her they were fine. While I made breakfast, she sat at the counter and talked to me. I asked, "Have your parents met Lon yet?"

"I brought him to visit a few months ago and they loved him. My life is finally beginning to make sense. I'm worried about my Dad, but the rest of the pieces fit."

I joined her at the table. We drank fresh coffee and ate Eggs Benedict and home made cinnamon rolls. I'm a good cook when I concentrate on it. The meal was a little extravagant but Kim had no need to restrict calories and it was a way to celebrate her three day stay with me.

Kim took her last bite of cinnamon roll, licked her lips, sighed and raised her eyebrows three times in quick succession, a playful compliment that made me laugh. Her phone beeped. She said "Excuse me," and spent some time texting. When she keyed off the phone she smiled but not at me in particular; it was a smile to encompass the whole world. "Lon," she said.

"Ah. I wondered about the glow. Things going well lately?"

"I think I'm going to marry him, Allie."

"Kim! That's wonderful."

"He hasn't asked me yet but we're both thinking in that direction."

"I'm so happy for you. So when's the wedding, and will I be Matron of Honor?"

"Problem is--I don't know if I'm ready."

I brushed cinnamon off my mouth. I felt wary of asking too much, wary of resuming a counselor's role with my friend. I said, "Well don't let him rush you."

"I talked to one of my friends about him, about getting married." She hesitated again, hid her expression by leaning her head forward to look into her cup, sip her coffee.

"And?"

"My friend says you should never marry your first lover."

"Your first? Lon was your first? I didn't know."

"My friend said you'll always wonder what other men are like in bed. You might think the grass is greener, be tempted to jump the fence and find out."

So, this was friend-advice territory. Reassured, I said, "The world is changing fast. A few generations ago, if you *didn't* marry your first lover your father went after him with a shotgun."

She raised both hands in a sort of affirmative gesture. "Some people still live by those rules."

"Yeah, and moralistic rules can be wonderfully helpful or very misleading but we still need them. Back in the later days of the sexual revolution, which I do remember fondly, a friend told me I should try sex with another woman. She said, 'Don't knock it till you try it,' like we were discussing a new flavor of coffee. It struck me as stupid and wrong."

Kim took her cup and plate to the sink and rinsed them before she put them in the dishwasher.

I began again. "I've never struggled with that decision, so I'm not sure what to tell you." She turned her back to the sink and faced me, still silent. I said, "I can't speak from experience but if you're in love with one man, could you really have sex with another just to find out what it's like?"

She didn't answer right away; then her expression melted into a smile. "Good question. Probably not. Although it might depend on the man."

I knew what she meant. Almost everyone knew what she meant. Hormones and pheromones don't exist solely within the bounds of love or marriage, don't convey the urge to mate solely within those safe parameters.

It was a heavy conversation for early in the morning, to go along with our heavy breakfast. I was still in pajamas and robe, padding around in my slippers clutching a second mug of coffee when my cell phone rang. What? Oh, it might be Betty. No, it was Amy Aren. Damn! Well I had given her the number. It must be important.

Her voice was loud, her tone pure panic. "Allie, you've got to come!"

"Come where? What's going on?"

"Chris is in the hospital. Please, I don't know what to say to him. I don't know what's happening."

"Is he sick?"

"They say he tried to kill himself."

"I'll be there in fifteen minutes. Wait for me." I didn't ask where in the hospital. They would be easy to find.

I drove to the ER entrance parking lot and located a spot near the wide, sliding glass doors. I got out, walked around the last row of cars and spotted Amy standing outside. Beside her stood the biggest, scruffiest, toughest-looking man I had ever seen, at least in this town. He looked to be about six and a half feet tall, a beefy two hundred and fifty pounds or so, with dark hair cropped so close it revealed his pale scalp and defined the curve of his skull. He appeared to loom over and dwarf the slight figure of the woman beside him.

I walked toward them. When I got close enough, Amy grabbed both my hands in her cold fingers. The big man turned to go. Amy released one on my hands to catch at his shirt. "Stay!" she said to him. "Please. This is my--my husband's counselor. Tell her what happened. Please. I still don't understand."

Amy's hand had wadded and hiked up the sleeve of the man's dirty t-shirt. A tattoo in Gothic script on his bicep read *No Mercy.* He pulled from her grasp and turned to look at me with eyes the flat brown color of frozen mud. I held out my free hand, the left one. Amy still grasped the right. I said, "Hello, pleased to meet you."

The man balled his hand into a fist and bumped my fingers, bending them painfully. "Bruce Woodhouse," he said. "Why do you want to know? I already told the police *and* her." He tilted his head down to indicate Amy.

"My name is Allie. I'm here to help Amy and Chris. You're the one who knows what happened--the whole thing. I want to hear it from you, directly from you. Please."

Woodhouse grimaced in assent. Inside the E.R., rows of padded benches flanked the inner wall to provide seating. Amy and I sank down so close together our thighs touched but the man remained standing in front of us.

He folded his arms across his chest. "Simple," he said. "I was having a few at the Wildcat last night. This Chris guy was there. Didn't know his name then, never seen him before. I could tell he didn't want to talk to nobody so I never went up to him. He's nursing his beers, one after the other, but not like he couldn't cough up the cash. He had a wad of bills in that wallet, more than one Benjamin."

I nodded, guessing a 'Benjamin' was a hundred dollars. The nod hinted at a crick in my neck from looking up at this guy.

He said, "We didn't leave 'til closing. And I ain't gonna lie. They can't arrest you for something you didn't do. I followed him. Was gonna boost him."

I didn't get it. I probably looked as confused as I felt.

"Take his money, Lady."

What could I say? I shrugged.

"Your guy started to cross the train tracks at Fifteenth Street, then he just stood there. The Three-ten was comin' down the tracks. I'm thinkin' he doesn't hear it or see it. I get closer and yell at him. He doesn't move. So I go right up to him. The train was so close the fu...--the damned whistle must have busted his ear drums."

Amy grabbed my hand again and squeezed it hard enough to hurt.

Bruce continued, "I reached out and jerked him out of there. By the scruff of his neck. His jacket came off. Buttons popped off his shirt. He landed with the soles of his feet barely clear of the tracks. Don't blame me if he got whiplash or something. I saved the damned fool's life. Now I gotta go."

"Wait!" This wasn't the whole story. "How did he get to the hospital?"

"I threw him in my pickup and drove him here. When I told the nurse what happened she called the police. She said he's *involuntary psych,* whatever that means. Crazy, is my take. He kept trying to leave and

I kept hauling him back until the police showed up. Now I really got to go."

I followed him out the door. I started to speak but he was already slouching across the parking lot. I yelled my thanks at his back. The rear of his baggy jeans and the heels of his steel-toe boots were the last I saw of him.

How was Amy taking this? A little breathless, I went back inside and sat down next to her. She was watching him out the window. She turned to me, shook her head but said nothing. Her eyelashes were dark with tears, her cheeks damp and mottled.

I voiced what she probably was thinking. "Unlikely Good Samaritan, isn't he?"

"He saved Chris. I'd give him a million dollars if I had it. Chris is safe for now, that's the important thing." She stood abruptly. "Thanks for coming, Allie. I've got to go, too. When the hospital called, I knocked on my neighbor's door and just shoved Buddy into her arms. She's got kids. I know he's okay with her but I have to go. Can I talk to you again about this, maybe tomorrow?"

"Of course." I stood and gave her a quick hug. Then she was gone. *That's it?* I thought. I didn't want to leave before I got more answers. I walked through to the inner foyer to speak with the volunteer at the information desk. She directed me to the E.R., where the nurse told me they had admitted Chris Aren to the second floor, general medical/surgical unit.

At the nurses' station upstairs, a middle-aged woman with a stern face told me the nurse in the E.R. had given Mister Aren the calming cocktail. I knew from my psychiatric inpatient work that the 'cocktail' was Ativan and Haldol a powerful sedative and an antipsychotic. "I'll just go peek in at him," I told her.

Chris would be in his room, sleeping off the meds. The staff would transfer him to the locked unit of the local psychiatric hospital as soon as they could medically clear him. They would take a CT scan of his head, do body x-rays to rule out possible fractures, take blood and urine samples. If he passed those tests and produced normal vital-signs, they would consider themselves done with him and delighted to have him out of their hospital.

I found the private room. It was small, unlighted, the curtains drawn. A woman in scrubs sat in a chair watching Chris, who was motionless except for the steady rise and fall of his chest. A sense of relief came while I watched his unconscious repose. At the same time, my mind rejected what I saw, or more accurately, what it meant. This was a big, healthy, intelligent, accomplished man, a teacher, a husband and father. He lay in front of me, helpless and unconscious, alive only by the strange convergence of two people with conflicting human intentions.

Had the "No Mercy" man, he of admitted guilt, saved an innocent man, or a killer? I realized I didn't want to believe that Chris Aren was a killer. A sliver of guilt pierced that reluctance. I had asked the same question about a different person just months before, in Yuma. My self-doubt led to actions that set a disaster in motion. I would not let that happen again. I had to talk to Chris Aren. When I did, I would know, without question. But I would have to wait.

Chapter Twenty-One

Halfway home, my phone beeped, signaling a text message. I refused to look at it or pick it up. I didn't want to know who it was or what it was about. No more input.

At the apartment, Zayd greeted me. Kim wasn't there. The dog padded into the kitchen after me and sank down, stretched out flat on his side on the tile floor. He watched me and I watched him. Nothing but his eyes moved while he watched me pour a glass of water and drink. Then I took out my phone. The text message from earlier was from Kim: *Garvin came by. Gone site-seeing. See you later. Thanks for a great breakfast!*

Nice of her to text me. I stood idly at the sink. I felt abandoned. Zayd looked listless, as if he did, too. I shook it off by taking him for a short walk. He perked up a little, while my thoughts returned to Chris and stayed there. Back at the apartment, I cleaned the kitchen, did other housework and went grocery shopping to provide for Kim's unexpected extra days with me.

Around four in the afternoon, Kim hadn't returned yet. Concern for Chris began to pull me back to the hospital. I didn't want to bother Kim with a call or text and I hadn't yet given her a key to the apartment, so I left it unlocked and put a note on the table.

***

One dim wall bulb struggled to light the hospital room. It revealed the same woman I saw earlier, still reading her paperback. She glanced up but didn't speak to me. I knew she was hospital staff, an assistant there to prevent Chris from doing himself further harm or attempting to leave.

At first I thought he was asleep but the sound of my footsteps opened his eyes. Unshaven stubble and a bruise on his left cheek darkened his face. His eyes showed as intense points of blue within the gloom. His gaze followed me while I pulled a straight-back chair next to the head of the bed and sat down. His focus shifted to the ceiling.

The situation was eerily reminiscent of my crisis-counselor days, when I often interviewed suicidal clients. It was no time for tact. I said, "The nurse tells me they're waiting for the results of the urine and blood tests. Then they'll transfer you to the psychiatric unit for a seventy-two-hour involuntary hold."

He didn't turn his head to look at me but said, "What?"

"In Arizona it's called *Title Thirty-Six*. The seventy-two hours doesn't include Sunday."

"Then what?"

"While you're in the locked psych unit, two psychiatrists and a social worker will interview you. If they decide you need to be there for your own safety, they can continue to hold you until they convene a legal hearing."

He didn't answer immediately. Then, softly, "Why would they arrest me? I haven't done anything wrong. I am not a criminal. I haven't committed any crimes."

"They won't arrest you. It's a civil matter. At the legal hearing, a lawyer will represent you. There will be an attorney for the State. You and any witnesses of yours, as well as the hospital staff, will have a chance to say why you do or don't need further psychiatric treatment."

He didn't respond, but I knew he was listening and absorbing it.

"At least one psychiatrist will testify at the hearing. The judge will rule immediately. If the psychiatrist advises further treatment and he agrees, he can court-order you for more inpatient treatment and up to one year of outpatient treatment. The court order would probably include psychotropic medications and out-patient counseling."

Chris shifted his head an inch to the side but he still wouldn't look at me. He said, "Well doesn't that just suck?"

"Not if it keeps you from killing yourself, it doesn't."

A tear slid from the corner of his eye and trickled down into his hair.

I said, "I'm going to get you a drink of water. Then I want you to sit up and talk to me. I want to know what happened and why."

The nursing assistant had been listening. She said, "I'll get it," put down the book and disappeared.

Chris continued to look up at the ceiling until she returned and offered him the water. He struggled to sit up, as if very tired or very weak. The hospital gown pulled down from his neck, exposing pale hair on his chest. He drank the water, handed me the empty plastic glass turned to look at me and said "Thank you."

I saw lines of brown from his temples back through his dark blond hair, where tears had carved wet trails.

He began to talk, so softly I had to lean forward to hear him. "The idea of walking in front of a train came to me...first came to me...it must have been a month ago. I thought about it a few times then after a few days, it wouldn't leave me alone. In my mind I could hear the whistle blow when the engineer saw me on the tracks." His hands clutched the bed covers. "The sound of the train whistle. It sounded over and over and over in my head. I started putting my hands over my ears to stop it."

"I never saw you do that, Chris."

He turned to look at me. "The psychiatrist saw me. He thought I was hearing voices. I told him I wasn't but he put me on antipsychotic medications anyway. And anxiety medications. I never did it again when anyone else was around."

"I understand. But last night? Did something happen that--that triggered you?"

"Maybe. Maybe the alcohol. I hadn't had a drop of alcohol because of all the medications, not since I went on them. Then yesterday I didn't take one damned pill. Later, at the bar, after I had a few beers, it changed."

"I don't follow. What changed?"

"The sound of the train whistle went away. The thoughts turned. To what it would be like after the train hit me. After I was dead. A sense of peace. Complete peace." His voice faded to a whisper. "It was such a wonderful feeling of complete peace." His features crumpled and his tears returned.

I gulped and reached for his hand.

He said, "I knew everything would be alright after I was gone."

That was it. He was done speaking. He pulled his hand from mine and slid down in the bed, flat on his back. His hands covered his face while his chest heaved with silent emotion.

I sat for a few minutes, trying to put together what he revealed with what I already knew. The med tech watched to see what I would do. I didn't know.

After a few minutes, I wrote my private phone number on my business card and put it on the night stand. I said, "Chris, I'll come to see you after they transfer you to the psych unit, tomorrow or the next day. Call me if you want to see me sooner."

I took the stairs down instead of the elevator. In that cold, hollow space his words echoed in my head, "...the sound wouldn't leave me alone...everything would be alright after I was gone...complete peace...I haven't committed any crimes...I haven't committed any crimes."

At the main entrance, I hesitated to leave. I sat on a chair by the door and took out my phone to call Amy. She would be home by now. I had to talk to her, go see her, the sooner the better. As I pressed in her number, a stream of warm air penetrated the air-conditioned chill. I looked around. The entrance doors had just slid open. They admitted Lieutenant Grozny.

Chapter Twenty-Two

Inside the hospital entrance, Grozny's eyes widened at the sight of me. He denied surprise by plastering a bland expression on his face.

I jumped to my feet. "Lieutenant Grozny. What brings you here?" The second I said it I knew it sounded stupid.

"Probably the same thing that brought you here, Davis. You can save me a stop at the nurses' station. Which room is he in?"

"You're not here to arrest him."

"Is that a question, Davis? Because it sounded like an order. I don't take orders from citizens."

"He's in no condition to talk to you. Can't you wait? Wait until he's transferred to the psych unit."

"You get to answer questions, Davis, not ask them." He turned and walked down the corridor toward the elevators.

I gritted my teeth. I wanted to yell at his back, *Yes it is an order, dumb-ass!* I fumed for the minute it took him to enter the elevator and the door to close.

I decided it was some small consolation that Amy was willing to talk to me. I made my way back to the parking lot while she gave me directions to their home. I stopped on the pavement near my car to catch hold of myself. No evidence of earthly chaos here. The spring breeze felt balmy. Ordinary noises floated to me on the air, background sounds of traffic and birds chirping. I looked around and saw sparrows flitting about their usual business. A squinting glance upward showed the sun cast the same golden glow as usual. It warmed my face, neither too intense nor too weak. Everything normal, as it should be. *God's in*

His Heaven and all's right with the world? I took out a tissue and blew my nose.

In the driver's seat of my Toyota Camry, I put the key in the ignition but didn't turn it. My hands on the steering wheel shook. It was past three in the afternoon and I hadn't had lunch. I decided I was okay to drive but I stopped at the nearest convenience store and bought a small bag of cashews and a tall can of Arizona Iced Tea. I consumed them, drove distracted, all the way to Amy's house.

When I headed to someone's home in Prescott, I never knew whether it would be a newly-built Victorian, a charming house built in the mid-eighteen hundreds and listed on the National Register of Historic Places, or one of the nineteen-fifties era, craftsman-built bungalows.

I found Chris and Amy Aren's residence in a neighborhood of newer, one-story ranch style homes. Amy came to the door before I could ring the bell. "The baby is down for a nap," she said, holding up a small white device, a baby monitor, the constant companion of the devoted or nervous mother. "Do you mind if we go outside to talk? I'm too upset to sit down."

"Of course," I told her. I was curious. I had seen her face sad and tearful but never flushed with anger as it was now.

She led the way onto the patio at the back of the house. The narrow concrete strip ran the length of the house. Several metal chairs and a long wooden work table furnished it. Beyond it, a tall chain link fence enclosed the lawn. I saw several pieces of metal and long wooden beams on the grass.

Amy said, "Chris is building a swing set--a play area for Buddy. It will be the best and the safest play area in the world." She turned to walk the length of the walkway with me at her side, then back again. Her stride grew longer and faster. I kept up but the pace not amenable to conversation. She was silent, intent, preoccupied by emotion while she strode from one end of the concrete apron to the other. I stepped back and sat down in one of the chairs, thinking I couldn't talk to her about Chris when she was this irritated.

She stopped and asked, "Have you talked to Chris yet? How is he?"

"I did, and he's going to be okay. Would you mind talking first about what's got you upset?"

She paused and appeared to consider it before she sat down in the chair next to me. She said, "Before you called today, a Prescott police detective-- Grozny, I think his name was--came to see me. He said...he said someone told them Chris had an affair with Carrie. Carrie Lougee, the woman who was murdered last week. She used to be our nanny."

I was stunned. Grozny must have come directly to the hospital to see Chris after he interviewed Amy.

She said, "It's a damned lie! Chris would never cheat on me." She blinked rapidly before she turned and looked into my face. "Would he?"

"Amy, I...."

Her voice rose. "Well, you're his therapist! What has he told you?"

I put my hand on her arm. "Anyone would be angry to hear their husband or wife was unfaithful. You know I can't betray a confidence, but I don't think you should worry. Maybe you can talk to Chris about it when he's feeling better That's all I can tell you."

She didn't answer. She looked at the baby monitor then put it to her ear. From a few feet away, I could hear it too, the faint susurration of an infant's breathing. She clutched the thing tighter and her hands sank to her lap. I looked into her face, trying to judge the severity of her emotional distress. I noticed a dark spot appear on her light blue blouse. It grew slowly. Breast milk. She noticed, too, but did nothing.

After a minute she turned to say, "Don't we have enough to deal with? Isn't he depressed and distraught enough without someone dumping crap on him? Our little Hailee...then Carrie and now this! Has the whole freaking world gone crazy?"

I didn't answer. Chris had asked me the same thing. I didn't know. I did know this was not the right time to tell her what I had learned about Chris.

She put the baby monitor to her ear again and listened to the hypnotic rhythm of Buddy's breath. We listened for a long time.

***

Back in my own apartment, in my kitchen, I told myself to focus on what we would have for dinner tonight, instead of ruminating on the day's events. When Zayd rose and went to the front door, I knew Kim was on her way.

When she came in, she brought the freshness of spring with her into my apartment. Color had brightened her face. She appeared energized instead of tired after her long day of sight-seeing. She greeted me then ruffled Zayd's neck and head, saying to the dog, "See, I'm fine. He's not a bad guy after all."

That sounded strange. I had to ask, "Did Garvin upset him, rile him up?"

"When Garvin came in, Zayd...I was going to say Zayd alerted, but that's not right. That only happens after a *find* command. He went into protector/defender mode. He didn't trust Garvin and I have to say Garvin didn't like him."

A sudden thought brought with it a pang of guilt. I said, "Poor Zayd. Maybe it's about being man-handled by animal control."

She frowned. "Could be. I'll have to watch his behavior around other men. Search and rescue work involves mostly males--law enforcement and volunteers."

We soon settled at the breakfast nook with a cool drink. Talking with Kim felt familiar and pleasant, as easy as reconnecting with a family member. "Tell me what you saw today," I urged, then relaxed and enjoyed her enthusiasm while she described her day with Garvin. He really had given her the local grand tour.

"So, what do you think of Prescott?"

She said, "Beautiful. So hilly. So many lakes. I really liked the downtown area, the courthouse square. Very traditional. Very different from the rest of Arizona."

"Prescott was founded about the same period in Old West history as Yuma but it reflects a different culture."

She traced the drops of moisture on her glass with her fingers but didn't comment.

I said, "In Prescott it was miners, Natives, cowboys and soldiers. In Yuma it was Mexican settlers, Natives, railroaders and soldiers."

"We shouldn't forget the prisoners," she said. "The film *Three-ten to Yuma,* about the territorial prison. The interesting thing about Prescott is a street they call Whiskey Row. It borders court-house square. Have you heard of it?"

"Of course."

"And a bar called the Bird Cage Saloon and other night spots. They have live western bands for line dancing and two-stepping."

I said, "I've heard. There's also a micro-brewery that produces different artisan beers, and a distillery that makes fancy whiskey."

She smiled and said, "Garvin wants to take me out this evening."

For some reason, I blurted, "Did he flirt with you, Kim?"

"He did. He's very sure of himself, isn't he?"

"So it seems. That's the charming side of him Betty told me about. I'm waiting to see--or hear about--the flip side."

She raised her eyebrows, then did that quick series of gestures for 'see, hear, speak no evil.' I had to laugh. She said, "Enough about the old guy. Tell me more about the great places you've discovered here in Prescott."

After dinner, we sat on the sofa to continue the conversation. I was determined to confide in her about the murder, the break-in and all the other recent events that had entangled and then confounded me. Then, there was the other issue I had only hinted at and wasn't sure was appropriate for discussion. She was young, single, an attractive woman who had been out with an attractive, single man all day. I remembered her comments about whether to marry one's first lover, and what she had just revealed about Garvin coming on to her. Where was their relationship headed?

Chapter Twenty-Three

Kim must have sensed my intent to delve into Carrie Lougee's killing, with all its mysterious nuances of circumstance. When we were both comfortable on the sofa, she said, "Maybe we need to talk more about Zayd and that murder you told me about. I feel terrible about the whole thing."

"Why for heaven's sake?"

"If I hadn't advised you to go back there, to the crime scene, you wouldn't have been arrested."

"If I hadn't been arrested, I wouldn't have realized how little they know."

"They don't have any suspects? And by the way, how was she killed?"

It was information I hadn't sought when I still preferred my head in the sand. I summoned the memory, which came quick and vivid. I said, "All I heard was the screams. I didn't hear a gun shot, so it wasn't that. Come to think of it, I don't know who called it in to the police, but a police officer--Officer Benson--was there. I don't know how quickly." My own words made me wonder, silently, *how did he get there so fast?*

Kim said, "What about the two guys you said Zayd picked out of the crowd?"

"One of them could have heard her and called 911, I guess. I wonder if Zayd did pick them out, or did he just find me and then....?"

"I'm not sure, Allie." She leaned back against the padded arm of the sofa, pulled her legs up to fold them at the knees, then drew her long black hair onto her chest and began to twist the strands between her fingers. A stranger wouldn't have known if she was a Native American conferring at a pow-wow or an East-

Indian woman practicing yoga. It occurred to me at that moment that I felt privileged to know her origins and simply enjoy her presence.

Her thoughtfulness gave me time to ponder the issue of confidentiality. I wanted to tell her everything I knew about the murder but I couldn't without revealing Chris as my client. It was unethical and could put me at risk of a law-suit. Still, this was important, life-and-death important, to cite a cliché, and I trusted her without question. I said, "Kim, the two men were Chris Aren--he's my client--and his father, Garvin."

She blinked. "Chris and Garvin were the two men? That's interesting. Garvin didn't mention a thing about the murder."

I said nothing.

"Well, I guess he didn't have any reason to." She hesitated again before she asked, "When we talked on the phone, didn't you say something about a baby in danger?

"Maybe I was overstating. I was thinking about Chris and Amy's little boy, Buddy."

"Why would he be at risk?"

"Their first baby was a girl who died when she was just a few months old--a crib death. Sudden infant death syndrome they call it now, SIDS. Amy started to have doubts about whether it was a crib death. Carrie Lougee was their nanny back then. She and Chris were in the home when it happened."

"I don't understand."

"I don't either. The coroner's report is virtually incontrovertible. They rule out every other possible cause before they call it SIDS. Why would Amy have any suspicion of either Carrie or her own husband?"

"So sad."

"Chris adored the little girl and they both trusted Carrie. From what Amy says, Chris was a great father--very involved. Buddy is about three months old now, the same age the baby was when she died. Besides all *that* stress, Amy is devastated because Chris avoids parenting the new baby."

"Is that why you're counseling him?"

"That and depression. I think I understand what he's going through. What bothers me is Amy's reactions."

"What reactions?"

"Today the local police investigator, a Lieutenant Grozny, paid her a visit. Evidently, someone told them Chris had an affair with Carrie. They wanted to know if the two were still involved when Carrie was murdered. Amy was outraged."

"Wouldn't most women react that way? Especially if they had no suspicion of an affair?"

"Sure. What Amy doesn't realize is that an affair would have given Chris a motive to murder the woman. If that thought was uppermost in her mind, the knowledge they suspect him, she'd be more shocked and frightened than angry."

"An affair *could* have been a motive for murder. It depends on the situation."

"I didn't say it was true."

"It still sounds bad for Chris."

"Garvin was there, too."

"What motive would Garvin have to kill the woman? Did he even know her?"

"At least casually."

Kim said, "If Chris committed the murder, Zayd might have picked up his scent on the woman's body, on the murder weapon or on things around the murder scene, even on the air. He air-scents, too."

That returning thought, the one that wouldn't go away, that my client could be a murderer, brought a queasy sensation. I put my wine glass back on the coffee table and said, "I guess it could have been Chris. That might explain some of the emotional turmoil he's experiencing. Guilt can produce that--lead to suicide, even. But Garvin was right there beside Chris. The same suspicions apply to Garvin, as well."

"True."

"And Benson."

"The officer? Why?"

"He was there before Zayd and I arrived. I always thought he arrived after she was killed, but maybe not."

Kim looked at me strangely. "I can't imagine what his motive might be. Isn't it likely he just responded to an emergency call-in?"

I had to acknowledge that with a silent not.

Then she said, "Chris and Garvin aren't the only ones in the suspect pool. You told me there were a couple of other people at the cul-de-sac when you first reached it. Since the police responded pretty quickly, any one of the onlookers could have been the killer, unable to make a get-away, just trying to blend in and look innocent."

"True, but not likely. From law enforcement's point of view, the best suspect is Chris. And me."

Kim said, "You're in an even more likely category. Benson found you and Zayd within sight of the crime scene."

My mouth closed very slowly. "And I went back there."

Kim put her hands on her knees and leaned toward me. "Tell you what. I'll ask Lon whether he knows anyone on the police force here. I know he's acquainted with some of the sheriff's deputies. Let's see if he can find out who they suspect, more details about how it happened."

"Like if they gathered any DNA or fingerprints," I said, trying to follow her lead, use my logic, deal with facts rather than indulge in emotion. "Maybe they're investigating telephone and cell tower information, things like that."

"Right."

***

On Monday morning, I felt relieved that I had confided in Kim and I think she was okay with it. We hadn't solved the puzzles we discussed, but now she shared them with me. What she couldn't share was the wormy feeling in my gut that I might still be a suspect for murder.

I got ready for work and put on my makeup. It was too bad I had to go to work during Kim's visit, but she said she would be fine on her own. She and Zayd might hike a little if her knee didn't bother her and she wanted to take a canoe out on Watson Lake.

Chapter Twenty-Four

I thought it would be an easy day for a Monday. My last client at two p.m., was a successful real estate agent whose picture I had seen in the Prescott Courier. Her chief complaint was a conflict with her grown daughter, with whom she was unhappy and disapproving. During sessions, she often used an annoying defense mechanism to divert the focus from her own issues. She would bring up information about neighbors or friends. I didn't relish the bits of juicy gossip and always tried to redirect her. I had to admire the fact that at least she never gossiped about her real estate clients. Her professionalism evidently made them off limits.

That day, we focused on appropriate communication skills and boundaries. Toward the end of the session, after I uttered my two-minute warning-- "It's about time for us to stop for today--"she uncrossed her legs and placed her purse on her lap.

She said, "Well, at least my daughter doesn't go for married men, like the one who got murdered."

I tried to swallow my swift intake of breath, but she heard it. Her eyebrows shot up. She said, "Well, I don't consider it gossip because everyone knows about it. Some women love a uniform. If you ask me, the most attractive thing a man can wear is a hand-tailored, linen suit by Angelico with a white shirt and a silk tie."

I gulped, tried for a neutral expression and said, "I won't dispute that, Beverly. I assume you're talking about Carrie Lougee."

"Of course. Her and that young police officer, Benson. His parents live next door to me and they weren't happy about *his* behavior, either."

I said, "Well, yes," trying not to betray the fire sparking in my mind. It took all my self-control to end the session calmly, to get her rescheduled and out the door.

So, Benson was having an affair with Carrie. Would Beverly have known if Chris was also having an affair with her? Maybe, given the social dynamics of a smaller town. But then, wouldn't she have named Chris, also, in her gossip to me? Damn! I could have asked for more information.

I despised these lines of thought but couldn't stop. If Beverly made the call to police about Chris having an affair with Carrie, wouldn't she have named Benson too? And if infidelity was a motive for murder for Chris, it was a motive for Benson. That made the officer significant for a reason other than my lingering feelings of resentment toward him. He had been right there, at what he called the crime scene. How did he get there so quickly, and how did he know it was a crime scene unless he had done the crime?

Virtually unaware of my body, I sank down in one of the easy chairs. The siren. Benson had arrived at the cul-de-sac in his patrol car with his siren blaring. Would he have arrived like that, drawing attention, if he planned to kill her? Maybe. If he was fearful her body would be discovered right away, or wanted it to be, it would be a good excuse for him to be on the scene. But while he was on duty and in his patrol car he wouldn't be on the scene unless someone first called it in. Officers respond to information and instructions provided by a dispatcher, not willy-nilly at their own whim. He wouldn't have arranged to meet her there to kill her unless he had an accomplice call in a report. The call-in happened *before* the actual murder? I mulled over that shocking idea. The timing would have to be perfect to blur the sequence of events in the minds of investigators. I had assumed someone else heard her screams and called law enforcement, but never considered it could be part of the murder plot.

It was too much to process. I told myself to stop ruminating and refocus. A breath of fresh air would help. I forced myself up and out the door. I walked around the block, carrying just my office key, like an ordinary person not thinking about murder, trusting mindfulness and Mother Nature to calm me. It helped.

When I returned, I snacked on crackers and an apple, then called Kim. She had just come from the Iron Springs Cafe, a picturesque red frame eatery in what was once a train station that features Cajun/Mexican fusion dishes, along with the ubiquitous burgers. She sounded very satisfied when she described the meal as *scrumptious*.

I smiled and asked, "Can you amuse yourself for a couple hours more? I need to go see Betty before any evening confusion sets in."

"Of course. No worries. I'll call or text you later."

***

When no one answered the door at Betty's house, I went around back and found her in the back yard. She sat on a green cushion in a large, white wicker chair in the middle of a small patch of lawn. A birdfeeder with a few moldy seeds at the bottom hung from an elm tree set among evergreens. An equally empty humming bird feeder dangled a few branches away. Several sparrows and a colorful grosbeak hopped in circles on the ground beneath the feeder, scavenging. A broadtail hummer buzzed the red spout of the feeder in quick, tentative swoops, then darted off.

Betty wasn't watching them, or watching anything. With her hands in her lap, she stared off into space.

She looked so vacant it frightened me. How much could I tell her of what had been going on? How much did she need to know and how much could she handle knowing?

I pulled a lawn chair over to sit next to her before she noticed me. "Allie," she said, reaching out briefly to touch my hand in greeting. "Come and enjoy Spring with me."

"It is beautiful today, isn't it?" I wanted to smile and breathe the fresh, pine-scented air like a normal person before the information I imparted might ruin it for both of us. I closed my eyes for a few seconds, then began, "Betty, it seems like there's something I should tell you."

"Oh no. Bad news?"

"Yes, I think it is. It's about the murder and about Garvin and Chris."

She interrupted. "Which is it, Garvin or Chris? Because we've already talked about Chris. I can't imagine what else you need to know. And a murder. That reminds me of something, someone with blood on their hands. And a drive by-shooting...from a golf cart."

I laughed before I could stop myself. "Betty, you told me that story."

"Are you sure? I'm surprised I still think of it. I hate violence and meanness. Like you do."

That was enough unconscious avoidance to tell me she didn't want to hear bad news. I patted her shoulder and said, "Tell you what, let's not even go there. When was the last time you had a cool drink? How about some lemonade or iced tea? I'll go get it."

"Right. Keep me hydrated. If I get a urinary tract infection, I'll be in even worse shape. Why do old women get mentally confused when they get a UTI?"

"I don't know but let's make sure it doesn't happen to you." I went for the iced tea and we spent a pleasant hour simply chatting.

At one point in the conversation, which concerned me later, Betty said, "I'm so glad Garvin is here. We've decided I can't afford to go to assisted living or memory care, but he said he'll be here as long as I need him."

I was sure she had told me just a week or so before that she could afford both those options. Which statement was true? I didn't question her but toward the end of the visit, I was tempted to broach the subject of Chris's hospitalization. It didn't happen. It turned out that Betty's unreceptiveness and my own reluctance was too big a barrier.

Betty's vagueness and self-contradictions concerned me, although she didn't show obvious signs of poor grooming or poor self care. I felt a little sneaky when I checked her refrigerator and took a quick look into her pantry to make sure she had adequate food on hand. Too bad my garden hadn't produced enough yet for salads. Before I left, I asked if there was anything she needed help with, then we washed and refilled the bird feeders together.

At home, I collected my mail and went to my door. The dog greeted me. Kim had brought him back and left again. I went to the counter of the breakfast nook to open the mail. One piece looked important. The business-size, imprinted envelope was from the County Attorney's Office. A thread of alarm stitched my thoughts. The letter was a formal demand that I submit the complete counseling records of Christopher Aren to their office immediately. I knew if I didn't obey, they would issue a court order. Then, most likely, they would subpoena me to testify in court.

Kim returned an hour later while I was fixing dinner. I wiped my hands on the kitchen towel and asked her to sit down. I didn't try to hide my anger while I filled her in about the order. "I won't do it," I told her.

"Why?"

"Because it's his personal life, his thoughts and feelings, his relationship with his work, his wife and his kids. It's none of their business."

"But if there's nothing bad in his file, why not?"

They're just fishing, looking for evidence to make him guilty."

"You're right. They're on the verge of arresting him but they need information they can take to a grand jury to indict him."

"How....?"

"Lon called. He found out quite a bit."

"And?"

"Blunt force trauma to the head. The killer hit her with a rock. Strangulation was the ultimate cause of death. Poor Carrie. They can't find a single enemy of hers. Not many friends or social connections either."

"Not unless you'd describe two married lovers as 'social connections.'"

We talked about the anonymous tip that Chris was having an affair with her, and I filled her in on the information I had gathered from my gossiping client.

Kim told me, "I also learned they looked at a former boyfriend and a previous employer she didn't like and quit. But Chris is their most viable suspect."

"Why? Do they have his DNA, finger prints, cell phone records that link them that morning?"

"He was at the cul-de-sac near the crime scene, and he knew Carrie, and they were having an affair. According to the tip, anyway. Ability, opportunity and motive. As soon as he's released from the psych unit, they'll probably arrest him."

"They can't have any real evidence. There's certainly nothing in my files--which they are *not* getting."

"Have you considered they might arrest you if you don't turn them over?"

"They can't arrest a psychotherapist who refuses to comply with a subpoena. There's a legal precedent for that."

Kim's face revealed doubt.

"I wouldn't give them squat, even if they did arrest me."

Her forehead creased. "So you said. You surprise me, Allie."

"I surprise myself. Isn't that wonderful?" I didn't wait for a response. "We can't let it happen, Kim. I'm more and more in doubt that Chris is the killer. If they arrest him for something he didn't do, put him in jail, it would finish him. One way or another, it would kill him."

Chapter Twenty-Five

It was a new me who set out to visit Chris the next afternoon. I was now an almost-violent woman, a scoff-law and would-be conspirator. I felt strong.

The local inpatient psychiatric unit is a medium-size brick building perched on a hillside that overlooked downtown Prescott. It can accommodate only fifteen to twenty patients at a time, a combination of men and women, court-ordered and volunteers. A mixed demographic and a usually low census contribute to a quieter, calmer ambience than one might expect.

I checked in at the nurses' station. The blond woman and I did a mutual double-take. It was Linda, the former charge nurse at the inpatient facility in Yuma, Linda with the honeyed southern voice and grounded personality.

I shouldn't have been surprised to see her there. Staff turnover is common in inpatient mental health. Workers learn very quickly if it's not the right job for them and move on to a different nursing specialty. Those who persevere become part of a familiar, collegial group who transfer jobs often as a way to reduce stress.

Linda recognized me, too, but I had to remind her of my name. After a minute to discuss our mutual relocation, she said, "You're here to see Chris Aren? His wife is a sweetheart. She wanted so much to bring the baby with her. I had to tell her no infants allowed on the unit. I think they're out on the patio. So many of our people are smokers. While they're inpatient, they're restricted to nicotine patches but the patio is still a favorite place. Let's go see."

She led the way down a hallway decorated with posters that depicted nature scenes. The unit's common areas we passed held furniture upholstered in outdoorsy shades of green and yellow. Through the large double doors at the end of the hall, I could see the compound featured a small patch of grass. I'm sure planners meant the decor and the compound area as a real taste of mother nature. It succeeds only if people ignore the ten foot tall brick wall that surrounds the outdoor enclosure, a not-so-subtle indication that it's a locked unit.

Two men and a woman patient strolled the perimeter together. Chris and Amy sat on a bench in the sunshine. Linda went back into the unit while I walked over to the couple.

Chris had closed his eyes and tilted his face to the sun. He held one of Amy's hands in both of his. They were silent, obviously comfortable with each other.

I hesitated but when Amy saw me she slowly withdrew her hand from his and turned to greet me. Then Chris stood and said, "Hey, Allie. Thanks for coming." His smile was warm and genuine. He wore the patients' dark green cotton scrubs uniform without self-consciousness. It seemed to me he was more at peace than I had ever seen him. Maybe the environment made him feel safe because it provided safety to others around him.

Amy motioned toward the far corner of the area, where a circular stone table with curved benches provided room for the three of us. When we had settled, she glanced from Chris to me and back. I saw his almost imperceptible nod of affirmation. She turned to me confidently, and said, "I told Chris about the detective saying he had an affair with Carrie. We talked about it. You know, I can read Chris. He said he didn't do it and I believe him."

Chris leaned forward with his elbows on the table. He said, "It happened just like you said, Allie--the psych assessments. But they didn't court-order me. I'm going home tomorrow morning."

Amy's quick glance of concern changed his expression. He said, "Well, back to my friend's apartment."

"How did you convince the psychiatrists you weren't planning to harm yourself?"

"I told them I never intended to kill myself, it was just an accident, because I didn't take my medications and drank too much beer."

"That's not what I understood, Chris."

He glanced quickly at Amy before he said, "No, it's not the whole story."

"Then I'd like to backtrack a little, go over it all again if we can so Amy can hear and understand, too. Is that all right?"

He hesitated. Then I saw his jaw harden. He said, "Okay, let's do it."

"So...when you were in my office last week and we went over the Obsessive/Compulsive scale. You remember that?"

"Of course."

"When I read the part about thoughts of harming your own child, did it hit a nerve?"

He closed his eyes and nodded. Amy's eyes widened. I caught her other body language, an almost imperceptible recoil.

I rushed to say, "Chris, why do you think that example was in the definition of the disorder?" I didn't pause for an answer. "Because it's so common. And so unlikely to happen."

Amy's frown told me she wasn't following. I took a deep breath and just told her, spilled the diagnosis like the gift I believed it was. "Amy, I think Chris has Obsessive/Compulsive Disorder. People with that issue often have thoughts about harming others that they would never follow through on."

Amy turned toward Chris. Her hand shot out to clutch his arm. "Is that why you don't want to take care of Buddy?"

He nodded. He hesitated, his lips tight, then said, "I would die before I would harm him."

Amy made the connection to his suicide attempt. She gasped. "Is that why you....?" Slowly, she reached for him and embraced him, her head pressed into the hollow below his neck.

I looked away. The other three patients who meandered the outdoor area looked at us. The emotion emanating from the couple's embrace sent them back into the unit. Perhaps their hasty avoidance was embarrassment, or simply tact.

Amy drew away from her husband very slowly, lingering in the embrace. Then she sat bolt upright and said, "That son-of-a-bitch!"

I started.

She turned to glance at me, then back at Chris. "Garvin, that son-of-a-bitch. Chris, did you tell her about him?"

Chris shook his head.

"He is a mean, sadistic son-of-a-bitch."

Well, that was a sudden shift in subject and mood. She must have seen my confusion. She shook her head. Then, committed to the explanation, said, "When Chris was only seven years old, Garvin got after him about some piddling little thing Chris did...Chris doesn't even remember what it was, do you, Chris?" He shook his head. Amy's fair complexion reddened with emotion. She was unable to go on. "You tell her, Chris."

"You know I don't like to talk about it."

Her stern look demanded it. He turned to me and said, "He put his pistol to my head. He used to carry it in a holster on his hip. He told me if I ever did that again--whatever it was--he'd kill me."

"No!"

"It happened again when I was nine or ten."

"He threatened to kill you again?"

"He wanted to teach me how to skin animals. He'd killed a rabbit. The knife was covered with blood from cutting off its head." Chris hesitated. He gulped before he continued, "When I told him I didn't want anything to do with it, he grabbed me and held the knife to my throat."

He hesitated when he saw the look on my face, then said, "I...I can still smell the blood on his hands, on the knife."

"Go on."

"He screamed at me...." The next words were barely audible, carried away on an exhale. "He told me I was a fu..... uh, a coward."

I couldn't speak. It was overload, even for me. This revelation was happening in the wrong place at the wrong time. Even so, I didn't want to halt its unfolding. I had to facilitate it.

I leaned forward and said, "That explains a lot, doesn't it, Chris? It helps me understand what's happening with you. The idea of harming your own child became real because of what your father did to you. But I have to ask...how bad are your thoughts or your urges to harm Buddy?"

He shook his head. "They come but I won't let them in. I run to shut them out, run until they're gone.

When I'm really tired, they fade. They fade to almost nothing."

Amy grabbed his wrist and looked into his face. "Is that why you just take off sometimes?"

He nodded. It explained a lot but I couldn't let it go at that. I had to determine the actual risk. "Chris, the urges--does anything specific occur to you, anything you've done or started to do?"

"No."

"No what?"

His eyes squeezed closed. "Once I thought about putting my hand around his throat."

"Did you? Did you put your hand on his throat?"

"No! I told you no! I would never let it go that far. I'd rather die."

There it was again, the reference to suicide. I stood, vaguely aware my bottom was numb from contact with the hard bench. I looked down at him. "Okay, Chris, that's enough! You need to understand something. Killing yourself is not a solution to this problem. Leaving your wife a widow and your son without a father...do not think of it as a solution. Do not think of it as an option."

Amy got up then too, paced back and forth a few times before she sat down and grabbed both her husband's hands. "She's right, Chris. I will not lose you. I *will not*." She turned to look up at me. "The medications he's on aren't helping. So what's the solution? What can he do? What can *we* do?"

"What just happened here is a good start. Understanding it. It's a fairly common disorder." I saw the doubt in her face. "It shows up in different ways for different people. You saw that old movie? The guy who's afraid of contamination and germs? Him and Monk, in the TV show. That's the obsession. Washing multiple times is the compulsion."

Chris stared at me. "It's not that simple!"

"Of course not. Those characters--most people--have a milder version of the disorder than you. Mine causes me to binge eat when I'm stressed. Some people develop addictions, like gambling. Compulsions and addictions can be two sides of the same coin. For other people, it's as uncomplicated as having to count things or organize things. It might have been like that for you, Chris, except for the...the trauma from your dad."

He only nodded.

"Then, the death of the baby. Those were triggers for you. They complicated your own disorder."

Chris and Amy continued to look at me as if wordlessly expecting more, wanting more. I said, "Okay, so, what's next? First, you need to have your medications re-evaluated. I don't think you need to be on an antipsychotic."

"Yeah. The medication makes me feel fuzzy and confused."

"For a person who is truly out of touch with reality, an antipsychotic is essential. It can make thought processes organized and lucid. But antipsychotics can make a normal brain vulnerable to abnormal, even psychotic thoughts. And of course, they can cause some unpleasant side effects."

Chris nodded again. They needed to hear more of what my mind raced to formulate. I said, "I'll refer you to a specialist in OCD counseling, Chris. And I think we need to find a couples' therapist you and Amy can see together from time to time."

Amy nodded.

I continued, "The most important thing for both of you to realize is that when Chris has obsessive thoughts he doesn't have to follow through on them. Obsessive thoughts and urges don't always lead to actions. Compulsions don't have to be given expression." I stopped, wondering if I had over-explained or gotten too technical.

Amy searched her husband's face. Doubt still clouded Chris's eyes. I told him, "Chris, you've already shown how motivated you are not to act on the harmful urges. Like running. It's a coping mechanisms. There are other coping skills you can learn."

He shook his head. "Will I ever be able to trust myself? Really trust myself with my own son? Will Amy be able to?"

"Yes, to both. Medications and counseling will help. Of course, you'll need to have agreements between yourselves, you two and the counselor and the psychiatrist, about the actual contacts you have with Buddy--when you're alone with him, that kind of thing. But over time, I think you'll return to your home and lead a normal life again."

Amy sent me a forceful glance then turned back to Chris. "We will deal with this together. Now that I know what you've been dealing with, you don't have to hide it. I'm not afraid for Buddy any longer, but I won't ask you to take care of him by yourself just yet." Tears sprang to her eyes and ran down her cheeks freely, tears of relief in the newness of hope. She whispered, "I can help you, Chris. We can fix this."

Chapter Twenty-Six

My mind was a whirlwind on my drive home from the inpatient unit. Chris had finally confronted his inner demons and Amy had recommitted to him, demons and all. Yet at any moment, police could arrest him for murder. Murder. A sudden connection stunned me. Carrie had been strangled to death. Chris just admitted he once had the urge to put his hands around his infant son's throat. Was there a connection? I hated the thought but I needed to examine the possibility. I mentally reviewed what I had learned about Chris's character. I thought about his struggles with him-self. I didn't want to believe my client was capable of murder. I couldn't believe it.

And Garvin! The man who was supposed to be taking care of Betty, the man who might even now be trying to seduce my friend Kim. What I had learned about him sickened me.

Riffs of emotion overtook me. I jerked the steering wheel right, slammed on the brakes and pulled off the road. The driver behind almost rear-ended me, blaring his horn as he passed. Kim answered my call on the third ring.

"Kim, do not sleep with that man!"

"What?"

"Garvin."

"What are you talking about?"

"You remember that conversation we had...."

"About being faithful to Lon? Well, so what? Since when do you tell me what to do?"

"Garvin is beneath contempt. It would be like having sex with the devil."

"That's enough. I don't have to listen to this."

She hung up on me. I wanted to throw my expensive smart phone right out the window. Instead, I dropped it into the cup holder, took a few deep breaths, steadied my trembling hands on the steering wheel and instead of going home, I drove straight to Betty's house.

Garvin Kastner's Trans-Am wasn't in the drive way. Good. Betty's 2010 Hyundai Elantra was probably in the one-car garage. I knocked. No answer. Betty had given me a key to her house the day I arrived in Prescott but I tried the door and it was unlocked.

The silence of an empty house stopped me on the threshold. I went to check anyway. Betty slept in her bed, an aura of deep somnolence in the room. Her clothes draped over the reclining chair. I stood for a long time, looking at her. I wondered what her dreams were like now, if they were different, if they were as confused and changed as her waking thoughts.

Finally, she stirred, saw me without alarm and slowly sat up. "Allie. I was just taking a little nap. What are you doing here?"

"Something's bothering me that I want to talk to you about. Let's have coffee. I'll make it while you get up and get dressed."

Minutes later, she came into the kitchen wearing a kimono-style, silk robe. Her face was damp from washing, her hair combed. I tried to smile at her across the table. When she had sipped half her cup of coffee I said, "Betty, why don't you tell me a little more about Garvin?"

"Like what?"

"What kind of work he does, where he's been all these years since your niece divorced him."

"I'm not sure I know all that. I do know when he was young he dropped out of college to start some kind of business--a tanning salon, I think it was. That didn't work out. When he married my niece, he was selling life insurance. Seems like that didn't work out either. He's had a lot of jobs since then. One as a security guard. He knows about guns. He likes to hunt.

"What does he hunt?"

"Oh!" Betty's face folded into creases. "I had forgotten about that. Once he brought my niece a dozen dead birds strung on a string. A present, he said. I think that really turned her away from him. Would have me, too."

My own feelings of disgust for the man grew. "Has he really helped you, Betty?"

Her eyebrows drew together. "He's been taking care of the yard work. He repaired my back porch steps. He's helping me with my bills, too."

A wedge of alarm split my thoughts.

She continued, "I have a hard time with figures--balancing my bank statement. After sixty years, I can't remember how to reconcile a simple bank statement. One more limitation with this damned disease."

I looked at my still-full cup of coffee. Cream-scum coated the top. I pushed it away. "I'm glad he's helping you, but would you mind if I have a look at your statements?"

"Whatever for?"

In spite of the question, she was perceptive enough to know where this was going. I didn't answer, just looked at her.

"Well, come on, then," she said, "no harm to check it out." She led the way to her home office in the second of the three bedrooms. It held an oak desk, two oak file cabinets and two chairs. She pointed to the task chair and sat down in the other to watch while I wheeled over to the cabinet.

154

It took only minutes. I turned to her. "Betty, there are quite a few checks here made out to Garvin. I thought he wasn't charging you to stay and help."

"He's not. Those are for Chris and his wife, and the baby."

"I don't understand."

"Garvin said they're in financial trouble because neither Chris nor Amy is working. He uses the money to pay their mortgage, buy food."

"Betty, I don't think that's true."

"A few months ago, I asked each of them, and they said they didn't need financial help." Her voice became barely audible as doubt assailed her. "Garvin said they'll accept help from him, while they won't from me."

"They don't need help, Betty. I've talked to them both. They're okay for now, financially. I don't think this money ever went to them."

Awareness overtook her, then confusion and distress. "Oh. Am I that far gone that I didn't see?" Her head dipped side to side as if in denial. Her whole body began to sway. Alarmed she might fall off the chair, I jumped up, went to her and took her by the upper arms to steady her. She leaned against me. After a few minutes she sighed, long and deep and looked up at me. "What should we do?"

"I think he needs to go."

"Yes."

"I'll take care of it."

"I need to lie down again."

I walked to the bedroom with her and pulled back the blanket. When she had settled down, I said, "You remember what you told me a few months back? That you found a wonderful company with a caregiver you planned to hire?"

"Before Garvin came."

"Tell me where the contact information is. I'll call and get someone here for you."

"But the money...."

"Don't worry about it. We'll cover it somehow. We'll sort things out."

She sighed again and closed her eyes. I went back to continue reviewing her paperwork. I don't have a great head for figures myself, but it didn't take long at her desk to see why Betty had been able to afford assisted living just months before and now could not. The checks hadn't been Garvin's only method to siphon her assets.

I sat back in the chair. His malicious intent and the extent of the deception weighed on my chest, stifling me. I had to get out of there. I jerked open the closet door, found an empty tote bag and pulled it down. I opened the desk drawers and file cabinet again, then stuffed the bag with what I considered the key documents, Betty's check book, bank statements and several other financial records.

For some reason my thoughts darted to Kim, Kim who might be with Garvin at this moment, Kim who had been my friend for years and now was furious with me.

I strode from the room, grabbed my purse and headed to the door. I opened it just as Garvin pulled into the driveway in the black Trans-Am. It gleamed as if fresh from a wash and wax. I went down the three steps in a daze. I stood paralyzed while he got out and walked toward me, smiling.

"The Bitch looks primed, doesn't she?" His mouth opened to say something else. I never heard the words. The desire to kill him shot through my mind and body, an urgent demand. My face felt unbearably hot. I began to shake. I heard my own words dimly through the sudden ringing in my ears. "I know what

156

you've been up to at Betty's. You will not steal another penny from her. You need to leave. Get out. Get the hell out!"

Chapter Twenty-Seven

Trembling but energized, I picked up the bags, strode to my car, slammed the door closed and drove home, too fast and barely conscious at first. When I reached my apartment door it was after four o-clock. I had to call agencies to find a live-in care-taker for Betty before they closed for the day.

I opened my door. The first thing I saw was Kim's suitcase, packed and closed. She stood near it by the sofa. Garvin must have dropped her off on his way back to Betty's.

Zayd rose and trotted to me. I patted his head. Kim stood and watched, silent. I started to say, "I'm sorry," but the words came from her mouth instead. I said "I'm sorry" too, blurted the apology to her before she finished. We looked at each other.

She demanded, "Allie, what was that about on the phone? That did not sound like you at all!"

"I just came from Betty's house. Let me tell you why Garvin Kastner is really there." We sat down on the sofa. After I told her about his thievery, I leaned forward to point to the tote bag filled with evidence of Kastner's theft. A wave of vertigo swept over me.

Kim grabbed my arm. "Are you okay?"

"Just overwhelmed, I guess."

I had never heard some of the words that tumbled from Kim's mouth. Then she said, "Allie, I didn't sleep with him."

"Oh, thank God."

"There was a quality about him that was just too...smooth. And I kept thinking of Lon."

"I'll be honest, that's a relief."

"Damn!" Kim's expression flattened. "Speaking of Lon, I talked with him just a few minutes ago. He thinks they're about to arrest Chris."

It was my turn to curse. "It just can't happen, Kim. I think Garvin killed Carrie. If he would steal from his sick aunt, he's capable of anything."

"It makes sense. From what you've told me about the whole thing, especially what Zayd did, it was most likely Chris or Garvin."

Incredibly, doubts rose in my mind, seemingly from nowhere. I said, "Unless it was Benson. Or Garvin. Betty says he knows about guns. But she wasn't killed with a gun. If Benson or Garvin wanted to kill her, wouldn't he just shoot her?"

"Good question."

"You know, if Benson was the killer, he might have phoned in that tip about Chris having an affair with Carrie. It would deflect suspicion from himself. Psychologically, it fits. It's called projection. You see in others what you don't want to see in yourself."

Actually, that was a stretch. My confusion was making me reach too far afield for explanations. Silent minutes passed while we tried to comprehend the unthinkable and find a way around the seemingly inevitable. I said, "We can't let them arrest Chris. He's innocent. I know he didn't kill anyone."

"How can you be so sure?"

I thought about it, remembering Chris's words, his face. I said, "I'm sure because I looked into his eyes."

Kim looked at me for a long time before she said, "Then let's think of some way to help him."

"Don't leave yet, Kim. I have to make some calls now but let's have dinner before you go. We'll order pizza. We can talk about it, figure it out later."

I was on my fourth unsuccessful call when she entered the bedroom with Zayd at her heels. "Allie, I think I can help."

I put down the phone. "How?"

"I can take Chris with me to Camp Verde on my way back to Yuma. He can stay with my parents."

I asked, "You'd do that for someone you don't know?"

She folded her arms across her mid-section. Zayd sank to floor, as if he anticipated a long conversation. She said, "I know him through you. If you say he's innocent, he's innocent."

"Are you sure your parents would be willing to get involved? I know how sick your dad is."

She came to stand next to me, her hand on the desk. Her fingertips drummed its surface. "When I explain it to them, they'll agree. They hate injustice."

"If the police really are about to arrest him they'll get a warrant. They'll put out a BOLO."

"Then Mom and Dad will hide him. For fifty years my father hiked and hunted for deer on our reservations and in the Chiricahua's."

I thought it through until I realized I was nodding like a bobble toy on a car's dashboard. I told her, "I think it will work. While Chris is safe with your father, I'll go to the police with what I know about Garvin." I grabbed her hand and squeezed it. "Wonderful--if only we can convince Chris to leave Prescott. I'd go with you but I need to stay here and take care of Betty."

"Of course." Kim blinked, tilted her head and then she began to laugh. Zayd scrambled up, opened his mouth in a wide doggie smile and wagged his tail as if he was in on the joke.

I wondered, "What?"

"Do you remember when we first met? I came to you for anger management counseling because I beat up some wife-abusing jerk. I believed I was an instrument of karma. Now you need to think about your own karma. I think *you* need anger management, Counselor."

I didn't have to think about it for long. I said, "Good point. I came very close to attacking Garvin." I had almost succumbed to a sort of behavior I hated and always tried to prevent my clients from resorting to. "But in my case, karma had nothing to do with it. I was out-of-control-furious. I lusted to kill the bastard."

Chapter Twenty-Eight

Kim called the local pizza joint for thin crust, three-topping pizza and a liter of Coke. Next, she called and had a lengthy conversation with her parents. After I got her nod of affirmation, I called and spoke first to Amy, then Chris. It took explaining and persuading, especially to Amy, about why Chris needed to go into hiding, but finally we arranged it. Kim and I were now co-conspirators, maybe law-breakers *hindering prosecution*, perhaps even *obstructing justice.* I had no qualms at all and it didn't dull our appetites. Between us we ate the whole pizza and drank all the soda. Zayd got the crusts, of course.

When we finished, I hugged Kim and her big dog one last time and carried one of her small bags out to the Jeep. Back in the bedroom, I felt jittery from too much caffeine and sugar. Again, I sorted through pile of brochures, notes and telephone numbers that Betty had collected about care-givers. It was a wash. It was well after five p.m. I would not find a care-giver tonight. When my mind cleared of that preoccupation, the thought of my elderly friend alone in a house with her thieving nephew gripped me. I shouldn't have left her there. Galvanized, I threw some night clothes and things to wear to work the next day into my travel case, and headed back to Betty's.

The Trans Am wasn't in the driveway. I let myself in and found Betty sitting at the dining room table dressed in flowing palazzo pants and a blue silk blouse. She must have known it was me. Her head bent forward, her straight gray hair veiled her face. She worked on a jigsaw puzzle featuring a bucolic Thomas Kinkaid scene, an English cottage with a thatched roof, smoke rising lazily from its brick chimney. Without looking up, she said, "Helps keep the gray matter from dying off so fast. This and crossword puzzles."

"Where did Garvin go? Did he move out?"

She said, "He didn't pack anything, just left. Didn't say where he was going."

"I'd like to spend the night here if that's alright with you. I can sleep on the floor in the office."

When she looked up her hair swept back from her face to reveal a discerning expression. "The recliner in my bedroom will be more comfortable."

While I found a sheet and a blanket for the chair, my mind gnawed at the idea that a murderer might live here. Where was he? More important, what was he doing and where was he that Sunday morning little more than a week ago, before he approached me at the cul-de-sac? Was there any way I could ferret out that information? A mental picture of Garvin formed. It wouldn't dissipate until it drew my attention to the Fitbit around his wrist. Of course, the Fitbit. The gadget recorded his every activity, sleeping and waking. With a GPS app, it also tracked where he was by longitude and latitude at any given time. If only I could look at it, it would reveal everything.

With little conscious intent, I walked into the hallway and across to the third bedroom, his room. I pushed the door open, closed it behind me without a sound and switched on the light. The room held a double bed, a one-drawer nightstand, a wall-mounted TV and a deep easy chair. The odor of sweaty sheets and after-shave accented the prosaic ambiance of the room.

I walked to the night stand without making a sound and slid the drawer open a few inches. It squeaked, wood on wood, unsettling as chalk on a blackboard. Not much in there, a nail clipper and nasal spray. I pulled the drawer out a little further. The gun stopped my breath. The black handle was curved for an easy grip. The grooved cylinder and barrel were silver-colored metal, with words carved into the barrel in tiny script. I leaned forward and silently read "Smith & Wesson."

I fought the urge to slam the drawer closed. Instead, I pulled it out the rest of the way, gritting my teeth at the protesting squeak. What was that, a deck of cards? Curiosity moved my hand toward it. Disgust snatched my hand back. The card sleeve featured a photo of a woman displaying her genitals.

Damn, where was the Fitbit? Well, did I actually think I would find it here? He was wearing it, of course, probably never took it off. About to push the drawer shut, I spotted something in the back corner. I hesitated to touch it. In another second, I recognized what it was--a dongle, a gadget that connects a Fitbit to another device. The dongle synchronizes a Fitbit with a second device, usually a computer. A one-time interface allows the Fitbit to automatically share all subsequent data to the computer. Did Garvin even have a computer? Maybe a tablet? If so, where?

I looked around the room again, opened the closet and carefully lifted things, pulled things aside gently to search. No luck. On a hunch, I went back and lifted the hem of the bedspread. There on the floor under the bed was a laptop no bigger in diameter than a large sheet of paper. If he had synched the Fitbit with it, this was a cyber-pot of information. I grabbed it, sat down on the bed and opened it. Immediately I was stuck. Of course I couldn't go further without a password. I tried his name with half a dozen variations. Then I asked myself what this despicable man loved, if anything. Of course, his car. The Trans Am. After three tries of variations on the name "Trans Am," I remembered what he had called it, "The Bitch." That was it. "Bitch 2015" got me in!

The wallpaper was a photo of an African safari, a White hunter with an elephant gun gloating over the body of a beautiful, dark-maned lion. Disgusted, I told myself to remember my purpose, keep going. Only a few icons superimposed the screen's background. I recognized one. It struck me like a blow to the gut. The icon was a green demon's eye peering through a peephole, the symbol for "Eye Like to Watch," a web site pandering to voyeurs. It featured sex acts and violent atrocities only a sick mind could tolerate, much less feast on. I had learned about it a year before from another psychotherapist involved in a criminal court case against a user.

Was I committed enough to continue? Covert computer hacking was not in my skill set. Garvin could burst into the room at any minute. The gun in the nightstand--would he try to kill me without hesitation? The stakes were high. They demanded caution. I put the tablet down and went to the dining room. "Betty, I'm going to ask a favor."

She reached for a puzzle piece. She picked it up and her hand hovered over the board with it. She said, "Anything for you, Allie."

"I'm in Garvin's bedroom, looking at some things. Okay, I'm snooping. I need you to come warn me if you hear him pull in."

She looked up, surprise on her face. Then she said, "Of course. I can do that."

Back in his room, I opened the computer again and spotted the Fitbit icon, a kind of modern oracle, an electronic swami that knows all and tells all. Holding my breath, I clicked on it. From the menu, I chose Exercise Calendar. Last Sunday, what was the date? After Zayd and I heard the first scream I had glanced at my watch. I was sure of both the date and the time it happened. I keyed in the date.

A graph filled the screen with data: when he woke and when he exercised or in any other way increased his heart rate. I compared the graph with the morning time line twice before I was sure. From just before the time of the first scream and for the next fifteen minutes his heart rate had soared. There was a short decrease, then almost the same heart-pounding rate again for more than ten minutes before it began slowly to normalize. What did that tell me? What could I conclude? That he was the killer?

I went back to the menu, found a Workout Share feature. It took a second before I realized what it could do. I entered my cell phone number and specified a text message contact. Whenever Kastner's heartrate was at the exercise level, the app would text me automatically. I searched, but what it didn't tell me was whether it also would alert him that I was the recipient, reveal me as a hacker. Maybe the information was there but I just couldn't grasp it, with my heart pounding and my mind running at fast-forward.

Did I really have the nerve to do this? I hesitated, drew a deep breath then finalized the application. A text on my phone would reveal him to me. I logged off and shut down. I put the dongle back in the corner of the drawer, careful not to touch the gun, and slid the drawer closed. I lifted the corner of the bedspread, wiped the smooth, black top of the computer with it and placed it back exactly where I found it.

The room was so still, so quiet. I took my green bandana from my pocket to wipe oil and perspiration from my nose and cheeks. I jammed the cloth back in my pocket and scrubbed my hands down the sides of my jeans. A touch at my ankle. I jumped. A scream

A KILLING AT LYNX LAKE

half-erupted from my throat. I swallowed it, looked down. Mange, the cat has snuck in with me. I picked him up, smiling, but then a sound penetrated. Garvin! He was here!

I ran to the door, tossed the cat out into the hall and turned off the light. Then I looked back at the bed. There was a definite indentation where I had sat. My heart pounded. I dashed back to smooth it flat, then raced to the door again, expecting to open it and see him coming down the hall or bump into him reaching for the knob. I opened the door. He wasn't there. He had probably gone to the kitchen for something to drink. I gulped and walked as calmly as I could into the dining room and sat down beside Betty.

She looked at me as if unconcerned but pleasantly surprised. "Oh, are you going to help me?"

I smiled at her, picked up a random piece of the puzzle while trying not to pant and gasp. I said, "Of course. I love jigsaw puzzles."

I saw a vertical line between her eyebrows, as if she was concentrating. "Garvin's home," she said. "Didn't you ask me to tell him something for you? Now you can tell him yourself."

"No, no, it's okay," I said. I felt something brush my ankle. Damn! I refused to flinch. It was Mange again, twining around my legs under the table. At least I knew he hadn't darted back into the bedroom. But where was Garvin and what was he doing? I waited for the sound of his footsteps coming into the dining room. What would another confrontation bring?

I glanced up at the door every few seconds but still managed to fit a puzzle piece, then another. After five or six minutes, I heard the sound of his bedroom door open and close, then silence. The tension in my body slowly ratcheted down to normal. I wondered if my thoughts would ever be normal again. What I had

167

learned in Garvin's bedroom and from his computer might not mean much to the police, but it spoke to me. I knew him fully, now. I knew all his names: voyeur, thief, child abuser, bully, murderer.

Chapter Twenty-Nine

For the next half hour, I felt like two different people. I was the shocked archeologist who had just unearthed a horrifying artifact and I was the ordinary woman calmly passing time with a friend. At ten o'clock, we left the half-finished puzzle to watch the news, then the monologue on the Late Show. Before eleven, we went to bed--I to the reclining chair. I had stuffed a pair of favorite pajamas in my bag before I left my apartment, but when I put them on, they felt uncomfortable. Maybe they felt inadequate somehow--or maybe I felt inadequate. The possibility of danger to myself and Betty was real in my mind, after what I had just learned. Of course I couldn't sleep.

When I knew by her breathing that Betty had drifted off, I eased over the side of the chair without raising its back, crept to the door and turned the lever on the knob. A locked door wouldn't deter an enraged or determined man, but it would slow him down.

He had killed, but why? His motive for Carrie Lougee's murder eluded me in all my previous speculations but that night it emerged with deadly certainty. Carrie had helped Betty with her finances before Garvin arrived. When she visited Betty more recently, Carrie looked at the records and realized Garvin was robbing Betty. He had lured her to the woods and killed her to shut her up.

Today, I wonder why I stayed there with Betty, with Garvin in the house. I knew a murderer could barge into the room at any minute. Why hadn't I taken the gun out of the nightstand drawer before he came home, and prepared to defend us both? The only excuse I have is that mortal danger was a force I knew existed but didn't really believe in, as if all lethal events and fatal outcomes happen to other people, exist only in stories, in fairy tales.

For the next hour, my mind circled in speculations. How would the police respond when I took Betty's financial records to them? More important, what would they do when I shared evidence from the Fitbit that Garvin was the killer? Around midnight, to still my racing thoughts, I picked up my phone and began to play Candy Crush. Half an hour later, I placed the phone on the floor beside me and drifted off.

***

I can't say what happened next. Not from my own limited perspective. I learned so much of it later, from other people and from newspaper stories. I had to come to my own conclusions about most of the extraordinary events that followed. Ernest Hemmingway--something Ernest Hemmingway said puts it all in sharper focus. He said, *"There's no one thing that's true. They're all true."* I agree with him, if what he means is this: each person's perceptions and their understanding of those perceptions form their personal viewpoint, *what is true for them*, their own, personal truth.

Hemmingway's assertion about personal perspectives will guide me while I relate what happened in all its disturbing detail. I have to include other people's versions of the story, told from their viewpoints. It's not so arrogant to imagine I can. Remember, I've spent years trying to get inside other people's heads, understand events seen with other eyes, comprehend thoughts sparking other brain synapses, then weave that information into coherent narratives understandable in the context of my own reality. Telling it that way will help me gain a better understanding of my own role in all that transpired.

Amy Aren. Late that Tuesday Night, Wednesday morning.

Silence woke her, the lack of a sweet presence beside her. Oh, she had not taken the baby to bed with her tonight. The doctors all advised against it. Silence. She couldn't hear his breath. Had the baby monitor stopped? The remote lay on the pillow next to her. She picked it up. No light; no sound. It was dead. Shock jolted her, mind and body. She darted out, around the corner and into his room. Shock turned to pain, exploded, and engulfed her. How much later she regained herself, she didn't know. She was lying on the floor by the empty crib. She scrambled to her feet.

In her room, she grabbed the phone from the night table and jabbed the keys: 911! When a voice answered, she didn't listen, she screamed. She screamed into the phone--again and again and again. Some time later, the sounds of sirens and pounding on the front door penetrated the noise of her own shrieks.

Later, she would realize it took only minutes for them to arrive, three uniformed men in two squad cars. She opened the door. They pushed past her. She went back to her room. She was dimly aware of flashlight beams, then house lights blinking on, voices calling, "Clear!...Clear!...Clear! She saw their guns first, two guns pointed at her while the third officer covered his partners. They entered her bedroom. One of them grabbed her arm. "Ma'am, what happened? What?"

She screamed, "Buddy! My baby! My baby! He's gone!" Her trembling hand pointed toward the nursery.

Both officers turned to go but in the doorway, Amy clutched the back of the second man's shirt and wouldn't let go. In seconds, he understood her and didn't struggle. She made him lead her, still clutching his shirt as if she were blind and helpless, into Buddy's room. It took only seconds for them to search it. The one whose shirt she still clutched, we'll call him Officer Smith, turned toward her, released her grip on his shirt, and let her head fall against his chest. He stayed with her, beside the little crib, trying to calm her. The other officers went through the house again more slowly, searching for the baby, searching for signs of a break-in, signs of violence. They found none. The lead officer called for backup. When additional officers arrived, they swarmed the home's outdoor perimeter, searching.

A policewoman appeared in Buddy's room, where Amy still stood in her nightgown. The woman went to find Amy's robe, then pulled her from Officer Smith's arms. She led Amy to the kitchen table, where a detective was already seated. Amy stood staring at him, uncomprehending. The questions began. "Mrs. Aren, how old is the baby? What's his name?"

"Why are you asking me questions?" she screamed.

"Please, Mrs. Aren. Sit down. We need information."

"I will not sit down. Go look for Buddy!"

The detective didn't stand, and he didn't go. He waited. The policewoman left, reappeared with tissues and a wet cloth to wipe Amy's face. Her panic yielded to that minimum of care, then slowly subsided a bit. She collapsed into a chair.

The detective's interrogation was direct but reasonably slow and gentle. Was anyone else in the house with her today or tonight? When was the last time she was with the baby? When had she put him to bed? Had she locked the doors? Where was she and

172

what did she do between the time she put him to bed and when she went to bed? When had she fallen asleep? Who else had a key to the house? Where was the baby's father?

At the last question, confusion swirled in Amy's mind. Had Chris taken the baby with him? No, of course not. He had called on his way out of town when the baby was with her, nursing, before she put him to bed.

The questions persisted. Where was the baby's father now?

She went back to the bedroom, the policewoman following close behind. Amy picked her phone up from the floor where she had dropped it. She went back and gave the detective the address of the friend Chris had been staying with. She didn't think to tell them he wasn't there.

The detective went outside to speak with an officer, whose squad car immediately peeled out and sped away. Within fifteen minutes, a radio message came back to the detective. The father, Chris Aren, had left late the prior evening with an unknown female in a red jeep. The detective needed nothing more. He called the dispatcher to order the alert. It was what Allie and Kim had anticipated and feared, but it arose from an entirely different scenario. It was a Be On The Lookout alert for the infant Christopher "Buddy" Aren, Kim Altaha and the baby's father Chris Aren. It was an Amber   Alert.

Chapter Thirty

Chris Aren, Kim Altaha, Kaska and Mrs. Altaha. Earlier that same Tuesday night.

It felt both unfamiliar and uncomfortable when Chris climbed into the passenger seat of Kim's jeep. The minor physical discomfort didn't phase him, although his head was within half an inch of the car's dome and he had to cross his ankles to fit in his legs. His unease certainly didn't involve Kim. Her manner was welcoming and calm, even matter-of-fact, although he was a virtual stranger to her.

In the car, he immediately saw the dog, harnessed and seat-belted in the back. He said, "Hey, big guy" and reached to pat the dog's head. A warning growl issued from the dog's throat. Kim said, "Zayd, calm down!" then turned to Chris. "Sorry. That's not like him. He's had some bad experiences with men lately. But honestly, I've never known him to bite anyone." Then she pulled away from the apartment building where Chris had stayed with his friend and turned her attention to the road and the trip ahead.

Chris was silent, thinking, *I'm on the run. I'm like an Old West fugitive, heading for a hideout.* Their destination was Camp Verde, once a historic army garrison and today a small Arizona town where people he had never met promised to hide him from police. He understood it logically but his emotions wouldn't reconcile with facts. Why did he have to hide? How could police suspect him of killing anyone, much less Carrie? How had he landed in this strange situation? The big hurdle had been his unwillingness to leave Amy and Buddy. They needed him, even though he couldn't be with them full time, not yet.

Things had changed in the past three days. Now Amy understood what he had been going through; now there was a plan to help him recover; there was a better life for all three of them in sight. How could he desert them?

Amy and Allie had pointed out that police hadn't charged him with a crime, so it was within his rights to get out of town. One thing impressed him more than all the rest. Allie said she knew who the killer was. She assured him she would be able to prove it to police. Then they'd arrest the guilty person and his life would be his own again, his to deal with his problems, to heal. She refused to say who she suspected of the murder; Chris just needed to be out of harms way for a few days. In spite of his trust in Allie, he wasn't convinced until Amy reassured him she and Buddy would be fine, it was the best solution for all of them.

The drive with Kim was uneventful. Before nine p.m. they arrived at the Altaha home, a little frame house in a secluded but ordinary-looking neighborhood. Chris thought it could have been set down anywhere in middle American, anywhere but on an Indian reservation. Then he asked himself what he had expected, a teepee in the wilderness?

Karen and Kaska Altaha greeted Kim with hugs and Chris with handshakes and the offer of freshly brewed coffee. Kim declined to stay. She wanted to get back on the road for the four hour trip to Yuma. Chris was grateful for the chance to sit and talk with the people who had agreed to be complicit in his first attempt to evade the law.

Both the Altahas were of average height and weight with dark hair and brown eyes. Their skin color was a shade darker than his own when he had a deep tan. Kaska Altaha's brown face had settled into the wide, tough creases of age and outdoor toil. His hands were square with large, straight fingers like Cuban cigars. To Chris, the man looked solid and dependable, indestructible as the earth.

When the coffee was gone, Kaska sat back in his chair with his hands on his thighs. "I'll say good-bye to my wife, and we'll get going. My folks had a cabin in Fossil Springs Wilderness not too far from here. Empty now. We'll stay there."

Altaha went into the next room and Chris waited. A popular song hummed into the empty time and the space in his mind. He didn't try to block it. It was harmless. His inner voice was persistent and often repeated song lyrics hundreds or even thousands of times over. Another frequent preoccupation was counting objects in a room. He had done that in any new environment ever since he could remember. Only now, he could count higher. A very high count would then lead to mental calculations in higher mathematics. He thought about his teaching and crash-analysis work for Embry-Riddle. When he was working, those symptoms of obsessive-compulsive disorder retreated, replaced by persistence and attention to detail which made him good at the work, earned him appreciation and praise.

Real sounds, muffled voices, cut through the lyrics and strains of music in his head. Voices from the nearby room sounded less like a farewell and more like an argument between Altaha and his wife.

Kaska appeared and nodded toward the outer door. "I already threw sleeping bags and food in the SUV. Time to go."

They got in the car, Altaha driving. Chris didn't like it, being a passenger again, being passive, dependent on others. This was not him. His only consolation was he was doing it for Amy and Buddy, that he had confidence in Kim, and now in her father.

Kaska drove with quiet confidence. He took Route 260 southeast, where scrub forest of pinion pine trees and alligator juniper filled the dark skyline and undergrowth of thorny desert chaparral edged the two-lane road. The hum of tires, heightened by the occasional vibrations and washboard racket of cattle-guards played background to silence in the car. The absence of male voices grew thick until Kaska spoke. "My wife is worried about me. My dialysis."

It took Chris a second to process the word. He said, "Oh. You have kidney disease. I didn't know. I'm sorry."

"I am too. Been on dialysis for six weeks. Hate it. For most people, it's a courageous way to live. For me, it's a cowardly way to die."

Chris turned to look at the older man again. His rugged profile reflected in the car window against blurred images rushing by. "Mr. Altaha...."

"Kaska."

"Kaska, we don't have to do this. I can't ask you to help me if you're not up to it, if your wife doesn't want you to. We can go back. No problem, no regrets."

"I never have regrets, Chris Aren. Once I commit, I commit. Don't ask me to go back on my word to my daughter."

Chris understood such a commitment to family, but his reservations about this plan for him sprang back into life. He mumbled, "I see." Silence again.

The road climbed. The increase in elevation brought them into a forest of ponderosa pine, gambel oak and quaking aspen. In Fall, the aspen would become a dazzling arena of gold-coin leaves dancing, shimmering with the caress of every breeze. Tonight the leaves were black slugs against the white bark.

Kaska braked abruptly, jolting Chris against his seat belt. A deer had leapt across the road, barely missing the SUV. Kaska turned to Chris with the hint of a smile bracketing the straight line of his mouth. "Her timing was good," he said. "Sometimes they jump right onto the car, like they're trying to kill it-- more likely, kill themselves."

Chris said, "It was a doe, wasn't it? It happened so fast I didn't even notice."

Kaska commented, "Lots of wildlife here, elk as well as deer, even some black bear. Glad we didn't meet one of them on the road." After a minute he said, "We're almost to the cabin."

The old Altaha family home was considerably more than a cabin. It was located in a five acre clearing, down a two mile-long dirt driveway through the forest. A three foot tall rock wall embraced three sides of the home. Beyond the wall was an orchard with apple and peach trees and beyond that an open meadow.

The three bedroom home was built to be self-sustaining, self-sufficient. A gas generator supplied the seldom used electricity. A deep well provided all the cold, crisp-tasting water needed. A septic tank serviced the plumbing. The little homestead had housed Kaska and his parents while he grew up and for a time after he married, it also housed him, his wife, daughter Kim and Kim's brother.

The SUV swung around the home and stopped between two pine trees. The moon was waxing, almost full. There was enough light on pieces of a stone walkway, even amid the surrounding forest, to make their way from the car to the house. Kaska Altaha slung his backpack over one shoulder and with the other hand effortlessly hefted a large, military-issue duffle bag. Chris brought the backpack that held his few current possession, and another bag Altaha had brought.

They entered the back door, which opened onto the kitchen. The room held a large wooden table and four wooden chairs, unpainted and scarred with age. There was no refrigerator. There were no doors on the wooden cabinets, just a sink and what looked like a gas stove.

Kaska went to a cabinet, reached down an old-fashioned lamp, its glass globe filled with gold-colored oil. He wound up the wide wick with a circular key and struck a match to it. A yellow glow flickered, then seeped into the dark corners of the room. "Have you had dinner yet?" he asked.

"No, we left in a hurry."

"Have a look around, while I go out and get the water and propane started again. Then we'll have a little something." He pulled several cans of food and a can opener from the duffle bag and went outside.

Reluctant, but resolved to allow himself the familiarity, Chris pulled a flashlight from his backpack and walked into the adjacent room. His footsteps whispered dust and desertion on the narrow-plank wooden floors. The living room was bare of furniture except for a long sofa of indistinct color and shape. Faint shafts of moonlight filtered through surrounding trees, penetrated age-veiled windows and illuminated the room with the candle-glow of a church sanctuary. He walked over to flick the flashlight beam into two adjacent rooms, also empty. That was enough. The rooms of the house contained no vestige of warmth or breath of habitation. Neither did they contain even an insinuation of danger.

In the kitchen, he decided the least he could do was prepare food for himself and his host. At the sink, he turned the tap. Air burped and hiccupped through the pipes, then a thin trickle of rusty water emerged and slowly cleared as it ran.

Kaska came in, shed his denim jacket, pulled out one of the kitchen chairs and lit a cigarette, leaned back and propped one ankle on the other knee. Chris thought the man in his repose, a stranger just hours before, looked like a friend, both tough and trustworthy.

The gas stove was an old model with white porcelain finish. Chris tried the first knob. It turned easily; the burner flared to life. They would eat warm beans instead of cold ones straight from the can. He found a drawer beneath the oven and pulled out a single sauce pan, wiped out the dust with his hand, then the tail of his shirt. He went to the table and selected a can of beans, the kind with a pop-top lid. He poured the beans into the pan and put it on the back burner, turned low.

He looked back and saw movement on the stove. A roach. A very large cockroach crawled on the back rim of the stove, closing in on the uncovered pan of food. His first impulse was to kill the thing. Somehow, this was different.

The insect crawled slowly, as if tentative or with effort. Chris aimed his flashlight around the floor and up the walls in search, but no other bugs, alive or dead, were in evidence. None joined this legitimate occupant of the house while Chris stood and watched. Drawn by the almost-forgotten smell of food, it came even with the pan and stopped. It was considering its options. Jump? A long jump into the pan of food. A short jump into the fire was a closer, more likely landing. Chris and the insect stood still for long moments, Chris resigned to accept the outcome. Finally the roach turned, went back the way it came, dropped from the rim of the stove and disappeared.

***

He woke to a profound silence and light so dim he couldn't tell if it was moonlight or the dawning day. *What is wrong with me?* was his first conscious thought. *What am I doing here? I belong with Amy and Buddy, not hiding out like a criminal.* He had tried to call Amy the night before as he lay in his sleeping bag on the hard floor. There was no reception here. He hadn't anticipated that. Now he wouldn't be able to talk with her, connect with her and Buddy at all until...when?

He had to go back. Even if it meant they arrested him. Arrested him for a crime he hadn't committed, a crime he abhorred, whose victim he had liked and still grieved for. Maybe Allie and Kim were wrong. Maybe he wasn't their main suspect. Maybe they wouldn't arrest him. Even if they did, even from jail, he would be able to talk to Amy, see her and Buddy now and then, help her get through this. Without warning, guilt rose to suffuse reason. He fought it, told himself he hadn't killed anyone, hadn't harmed anyone, but oh, his thoughts, the unspeakable suggestions that had risen, seemingly from the depths of Hell, to torment his mind. What appalling conditions this accursed mental illness had brought into their lives! He scrubbed at his face with harsh hands. From somewhere came a thought, seemingly in Allie's words, Allie's voice. Wallowing in guilt was self-indulgent. He couldn't let it overtake him, turn him into a coward, self absorbed in his own misery. His wife and baby were what mattered, who and what he had to take care of. He tamped down his emotions, steeled his mind against unbidden thoughts and crawled out of the sleeping bag. He was sore and stiff, sleepy and hungry, but determined. He used the bathroom, then went to wake his host.

Chapter Thirty-One

(Me) Allie Davis and Betty Jackson, early hours of Wednesday morning.

A noise startled me awake, a loud, warbling tone from my phone. I grabbed it, frantically pressed the volume button. The noise didn't diminish.

Betty roused. "What is that, Allie?"

"Nothing, just my phone. Sorry. Go back to sleep, Sweetie." Betty's head sank down to the pillow again.

I unlocked the bedroom door and stepped into the hall while I looked at the message scrolling across the phone. "*Amber Alert.*" It was law enforcement's automatic notification of a missing child, an electronic message sent to all citizens reachable via a communication device.

Detailed information began to appear. "The infant is believed to be with his father and an unidentified female in a late-model, red jeep, Arizona license number - - - - - -." I gasped. That was Kim's jeep. They were after Kim and Chris!

I watched the message repeat, uncomprehending. Had Chris and Kim taken the baby with them? The message stopped. I stood, blinking at the phone, trying to absorb the information. Another sound from the phone, much softer, startled me. It was a text message from Kastner on the "Exercise Share" app. I struggled to refocus, opened the app and studied the graph. For the last hour, Kastner's heart rate had soared, dipped, soared again, and fifteen minutes before now, returned to normal.

For some reason, my knees grew weak. With my back against the wall, I slid to the floor, still staring at the phone. I tried to dismiss it. There was too much information here. The Amber Alert was more important. I told myself to figure out what that meant.

Finally, two seemingly unrelated pieces of information from entirely different sources meshed, to form a coherent explanation. I resisted it. It was too horrible. But Betty had told me Garvin had a key to Chris and Amy's house. Chris had given it to his father. Garvin Kastner had access to the Aren home. What did I know about Kastner? That he was capable of the worst conceivable human behaviors, had terrorized his own young son. Now Kastner had kidnapped his own grandchild. He had kidnapped the baby and--done what with him? I refused to let my mind go there. I pressed my back against the wall and, with protesting knees, pushed up to stand again. I had to resist, to summon my strength, my will to do something, anything to fix this, change this. My chin sank toward my chest. I was only dimly aware when tears began to drop onto my bare toes.

A frisson of anger, then alarm shot up my spine. Kastner's heart rate had returned to normal. Where was he right now? He was in his room when Betty and I went to bed. Had he returned? I peeked around the corner, down the hallway toward his door. A strip of light showed on the floor. I had to know. Thoughts of my own safety didn't exist. I would kill him with his own gun if he was there. I walked down the hall and pushed open the door. His bed was rumpled but empty. I went to the nightstand and pulled open the drawer. The gun was gone.

A sound intruded, an incoming call on the phone in my hand. Kim was trying to call me. Kim had heard the Amber Alert, too.

"Allie, what the hell?"

"Kim, where are you?"

"Highway 85, almost to Gila Bend," she said. "On the outskirts of Camp Verde I stopped at a friend's house and talked for a while. If I hadn't, I'd be home by now."

"Every law enforcement officer in the state is looking for you!"

"I know, but I've got nothing to hide. He's not with me, you know that. What is this? Who took him?"

"Wait, let me go back to my room--the room." A few steps took me back to Betty's bedroom, where I closed the door and locked it again. When Kim had left me that evening, I was safe in my apartment. I didn't waste time to explain where I was or what I had been doing. I hoped she wouldn't ask.

I blurted, "Garvin did it. I don't want to explain how I know, but it was Garvin."

"Then we need to find them."

"What do you mean, *we*? The police are looking for Buddy. The State police are looking for him. The FBI is looking for him, or they may be soon. You need to go turn yourself in and make them understand."

"No."

"Kim!"

"Allie, they're looking for me, and I don't have him. You forget who I am. You forget what Zayd and I do. We're search and rescue. I'm coming back there. Get me something with Garvin's scent on it and something with the baby's scent."

"Where are you right now?"

"I told you, near Gila Bend. Oh...I pulled off onto a side road. I'm down in a deep gulley off the shoulder."

"You know if you get back on the highway, they'll find you, they'll stop you."

"Damn! You're right. I'm pretty well hidden where I am. I just let Zayd out to do his business. We're hunkered down again."

"Then stay there! I'll get the scent items and come get you. Nobody's looking for me and my car."

"You sure...."

"For heaven's sake! Skip it."

"Okay. Pull on rubber or nitrile gloves before you collect the scent things. Put them in different Ziploc bags, each in two bags, and one inside the other."

"Kim, what if they're monitoring your phone?"

"Oh. I'm not sure they could--at least not this fast. When you get close, call me. I'll give you directions without identifying exactly where we are."

"It'll take time to wake Betty and get her somewhere safe. Then I'll go to the Aren house for something of Buddy's. I can't get to you in less than-- maybe three hours."

"Whatever. I'm not budging. Zayd is a fairly comfy pillow. We'll take a nap."

"Kim!"

"What?"

"You're the only person who could even *think* of sleep right now." I heard Kim's soft laugh before I ended the call. I chuckled a little myself, my voice wavering, fright-or-flight chemicals surging.

Most of the next hour remained a blur of frenzied activity. I went to Kastner's bathroom, opened the hamper, picked up a soiled t-shirt with latex-gloved hands and stuffed it into plastic bags, then crammed it into my canvas tote. I packed a few things for Betty in a small suitcase I found in the closet, then woke her. What I said to persuade her we had to go, I don't remember. What stuck in my mind was what she said, her frantic cry when she was safe at last in my car, "Mange, Mange!"

"What?" Then I raced back into the house. The cat had been roused by all the activity and decided on an early breakfast. I started to pick him up, but wary of his claws, grabbed a dish towel and wrapped it around him before I snatched him away from his food dish. I cradled the towel-wrapped cat in both arms, ran to the car and dropped him into Betty's lap. My pulse pounding in my throat, I got in, switched on the engine and headlights, and pulled away from the curb in the darkness. Betty held the cat and demanded. *"What is going on?"*

Seconds later, a block from the house, Garvin passed is in his Trans Am. If we had delayed a minute more, he would have intercepted us. What I knew about him and what my imagination conjured transformed his face into that of a demon in my frantic mind. The sinister black car driven by a demon was the memory encoded in my brain forever, implanted there by fearful stimuli. It was what psychologists call a *negative valence*. The image faded as I drove. Half way to my apartment, I remembered. Kastner knew where I lived and he saw us run. We couldn't go home.

Some time after two a.m., I checked into a hotel on Highway 69-South. The clerk at the desk was sleepy and slow to understand I wanted two queen sized beds instead of one king size, and ground floor instead of third floor. Betty stayed in the car with the cat while I walked through the lobby with her bag, under the obligatory inspection of the clerk. When I had the lights on in the room and the heater set, I went to get Betty and the cat. I brought them in through the door at the end of the corridor, hoping the security cameras wouldn't identify the bundle in my arms as a cat. Mange aided the subterfuge by not yowling.

Inside, it took a few minutes before Betty was settled. I dialed 911. The female dispatcher informed me in an aggrieved tone bordering on rude, that a case of elder financial abuse was not an emergency.

Trying to remain calm, I said, "You don't understand. His name is Garvin Kastner. He has a gun! He kidnapped the Aren baby. I think he murdered Carrie Lougee."

"Wait Ma'am. Slow down," the woman said. "What's your name?"

I repeated it, then, "Talk to Lieutenant Grozny. He knows my name. Tell him to bring someone from Victim Witness Services for my friend Betty Jackson. She has memory problems and this is very traumatic for her. She needs support. Tell Lieutenant Grozny I'll explain it all when he gets here."

It was a lie. I had no intention of staying. I knew one or more police officers would arrive within minutes. Grozny might or might not be with them, but I was sure they would bring a trained human services worker to take care of Betty.

Betty had been listening. She sat down on the bed, her face blank with shock. She had heard and understood it all. She reached for my hand.

I had to tell her, "I have to go now, Betty. I know this is hard for you, but I need you to stay here. You'll be safe here."

She surprised me. She said, "Of course. Don't worry about me. I don't know what you're up to but be careful."

It took less than ten minutes to drive to the Aren home. I pulled the car up to the curb behind two police vehicles and managed to walk past them unchecked. At the door, two officers stopped me and began to ask questions. I gave them my name and said, "I'm Amy's friend." Knowing the words meant the same but one sounded more impressive, I said, "I'm a psychotherapist."

Amy was sitting in the living room with a uniformed officer. She saw the commotion and yelled to them, "Let her in!"

When I stepped inside, she rushed into my arms. We walked to the sofa, still clutching each other. I glanced at the uniformed officer who had followed us. He now stood a respectful eight or ten feet away. I turned back to Amy and lowered my voice, "Amy, listen! Don't talk. Just listen. I know what happened. We'll find him. I'm going to leave in a minute, but I promise we'll find him."

She stared at me. "How?"

I frowned, whispered, "Shhh."

In a lower voice she said, "Oh, I don't care. Find him. Please!"

I sat with her a few minutes more before I stood and said to the officer, "The bathroom. I have to go." He just nodded. He remained watching Amy while I found the bathroom. Its door was out of sight from the living room. I slipped back out and found my way to the baby's room. Buddy's blue pacifier lay in the corner of his empty crib. Fighting back emotion, I collected it as Kim had instructed and put it in my purse.

Now I had what Kim needed, I had an impulse to run through the back door and race to my car. There were too many police around. I couldn't risk rousing their suspicion. I forced myself to walk back to the living room and sit again with Amy on the sofa. Then it occurred to me--what if we didn't? I had as much as promised Amy we would find the baby. What if we couldn't?

After minutes that seemed like hours, I said, loud enough for the officer to hear, "I really have to go now, Amy, but you can call me if you need me." Holding my breath, I rose and walked out. The officer at the door didn't stop me. The one on duty outside next to his patrol car eyed me but didn't try to stop me as I walked past him. I got into my car and drove away.

The adrenalin began to wear off. I had slept only two hours, but I didn't stop for coffee until I reached Spring Valley, near the intersection of a major Central Arizona artery, Highway 17. The divided highway, two lanes on each side, would take me down the ridges of the Bradshaw mountains, over the Mogollon Rim, around the sprawling Phoenix metropolitan area and onto Highway 85 near the desert town of Gila Bend. There, somehow, I would find Kim.

Chapter Thirty-Two

Grady Brown and Buddy Aren. Early Wednesday morning.

Grady couldn't wait for his first solo in the Piper Arrow today. Lift-off at 6:00 a.m.! His Embry-Riddle instructor would be there, of course, to observe from the ground, and his parents in Juneau, Alaska, were most likely already waiting for his face-time phone call to say he had made it and was now a licensed pilot.

It was around 5:00 a.m. when he left the small apartment he shared with two other students. He drove directly to the flight line, adjacent to Prescott Municipal Airport. His instructor wouldn't have arrived yet, but he wanted a little alone time before the flight. The flight line included more than ten acres of tarmac, where "ERAU" was inscribed in huge letters on the University's buildings and runways. Up to thirty airplanes and ten helicopters could be housed or parked on the lot. His Piper was outside, on the tarmac at the lower end of the complex, its cockpit hooded against the intense sunlight and often blustery mountain weather.

Grady parked in the student lot and strode toward the plane, thinking only of the anticipated flight, his solo flight. Nearing the plane, he stopped. Shock. The canopy was bare. Rays of sun mounting the ridge of Thumb Butte reflected off the dome into his eyes. What happened to the cover? *And what was that? Shit!* Was he hallucinating? It sounded like a baby. A baby crying. The sound came from inside his training plane, from inside his Piper.

***

(Me) Allie, Kim, Chris, and Kaska. Wednesday morning.

What coincidence, what peculiar force of synchronicity set the arrival of Kim and me, Chris and Kaska, in the slowly awakening town of Prescott at virtually the same moment? What power inspired the elaborate choreography that brought us together? Some might say it was serendipity. Pragmatists would say it was the inevitable consequence of individual decisions made by each of the players in the drama. Others would insist it was God's work at a time he chose to remain anonymous.

***

Minutes before Chris and Kaska entered the city, Chris finally got reception on his phone. Amy answered on the fourth ring, her voice a weak whisper. Startled, he said, "What's wrong? Your voice...."

"I think it's from screaming. Where have you been? Why couldn't I reach you? I've been trying to call you! Buddy is fine."

"Screaming? Amy! Are you alright?"

Amy whispered that yes, she was okay.

"I've been trying to call you, too," Chris said. "There was no reception. It's the main reason I decided to come back. Are you at home?"

Amy told him she was at the hospital with Buddy. The baby was cranky from lack of sleep but doctors had checked him, medically cleared and released him and now she was nursing him--trying to nurse him-- before they left. The police were going to drive them home. They would finally get some sleep.

Chris was more than confused; he felt disoriented. He said, "I don't understand. What happened?"

Amy sighed, and slowly, with many interruptions by Chris, explained. Only then, in the same harrowing moments, Chris learned his son had been kidnapped, then found safe and unharmed three hours later. It was the greatest shock followed by the greatest relief of his life.

When he was sure she had said all she could, he said, "I'm coming home. I'll be there in ten or fifteen minutes."

I had been trying to call Chris. The second he keyed off his phone call with Amy, mine went through. I said, "Chris, Amy called me. The baby is safe!"

He said, "I know. I just spoke to her."

"You know Kim didn't take him?"

"Of course not. Why would she do that?"

"Where are you now?" I asked. "Still with Mr. and Mrs. Altaha?"

"I'm in Prescott. I can't stay away from Amy and Buddy. We're on our way there now."

I raised my voice. "Don't do that, Chris! There's a BOLO out for Kim and you, for kidnapping the baby. If you show up, they'll arrest you. I know something that can clear you. You've got to believe that. I'm headed back right now to talk to the police."

"Why would they think I kidnapped Buddy? It's ridiculous! Why the hell am I the suspect again?"

"You left town last night around the time he was taken. Damn, it doesn't matter why they're after you. If you stay out of sight for another hour or two we can get you cleared of this mess."

Chris hesitated. He said, "Amy told me they found him at the Embry-Riddle flight line. It doesn't make sense!"

I told him, "It makes sense to me. I know this will be hard for you to hear, Chris, but I think Garvin kidnapped the baby. He put Buddy in the plane to divert suspicion from himself, turn it back onto you."

Silence.

I said, "I think he murdered Carrie."

Chris turned to Kaska. "Stop the car."

Kaska Altaha was a man not used to taking orders and not given to swift reaction but he had overheard much of the conversation and saw an alarming tension rising in the young man his daughter had entrusted to his care. He pulled the SUV into a nearby fast-food restaurant parking lot.

Chris said to him, "Sorry, that was rude. I need to talk to her. It won't take long." To me, he said, "I told you my dad did some fairly despicable things when I was young and you probably don't like him much, but I can't believe he would...."

"Chris, I've got the proof. I really do."

Silence. Then he said, "I will kill him."

Kaska had been looking discreetly out the window. He turned. I didn't know it then, but he could hear my voice from the phone and he listened to both sides of the conversation that followed.

I said to Chris, "You will not kill anyone! The police will take care of him."

"If he's got even an hour's lead, the police will never catch him."

"Why? Why would you say that?"

"He considers himself a survivalist. He's prepared to be a fugitive. I've seen him make plans. If he's not at Betty's house, I know where he would go."

"Where?" I didn't wait for his response. "So, call the police. Tell them."

He said, "I couldn't tell them exactly where. I'm not sure I could find it myself."

I was growing more frustrated by the second. I asked, "So, where would he go?"

"Down by Lynx Lake, somewhere near the east shore. It's a fox-hole. Actually, it's small, more like a spider hole. He camouflaged it over. He stores survival gear there, a phony I.D., a passport, cash, and a rifle."

I think I snorted. It was a sound of disgust. I said, "I'm not surprised. Still, you should lay low and take care of yourself. Amy and Buddy are safe but the police will still be at the house."

Chris grew silent, pondering. He needed to be with Amy, comfort Amy, hold his infant son. With that thought, he realized the prospect of holding Buddy produced no anxiety, no fear, no intrusive thoughts or images.

I questioned his silence. "Chris, are you there?"

He said, "I guess you're right. I shouldn't go home now."

"Good. I have to go check on Betty. We'll talk later, okay?"

"Sure." Chris let his hand with the phone slowly settle to his knee while he struggled to comprehend a world gone berserk. He turned to Kaska. "You've done so much for me already, Kaska. But would you drive me to Lynx Lake instead of to my house? I have to find someone. I'll give you directions there."

Kaska regarded him with a blank face. "What are you going to do when you find this person?"

Chris realized Kaska had been listening and knew the gist of the situation. He considered the question for only seconds. "If he's there, I'll hold him until the police come to get him. If he's not, I'll take what he stored down in the hole. Especially the gun. I can't let him use the gun."

Kaska nodded. He appeared unfazed and accepting. He turned the car. They headed back, out of town in the other direction, toward Lynx Lake.

Chapter Thirty-Three

Me (Allie), Kim, Betty and Lieutenant Grozny. Wednesday morning.

I grasped the steering wheel even tighter. I turned to Kim. She was seated next to me, while Zayd occupied the length of the back seat. I said, "You heard most of the conversation, didn't you?"

Kim nodded. "I'm so glad the baby is safe. The thought of giving Zayd the sent command for a kidnapped infant is my worst nightmare. It's something I've never had to do and hope I never will. But Garvin...."

"Yeah. He's dangerous. Chris and your Dad...."

Kim finished my sentence, "...are going to look for him. I need to be there, too. And you need to be with Betty. After we get to the hotel, let me take the car. Zayd and I have to go to Lynx Lake. If Chris and my dad can't find Kastner, Zayd will."

***

It was around six-thirty a.m. when I pulled into the parking lot of the hotel. When I released my grip on the steering wheel, my painful knuckles told me I had been clutching it. I leaned back in the seat and turned to Kim. She said, "You saved me." She glanced into the back seat, where Zayd now sat on his haunches, expecting finally to be let out of the car. She added, "You saved *us*."

I took a deep breath. I felt too tired to think clearly but I heard myself say, "Karma at work again."

She smiled at me. "You're here, a hotel. Go rest." She got out and came around to the driver's side.

I felt the stiffness in my limbs from hours of sitting when she grabbed and hugged me. "Be careful," I said. "You and Zayd." I watched her drive away.

At the hotel door, I slid the plastic key card into the slot Who would I find here and what would happen next, considering the way I left? The second the door swung open, I felt the emptiness. No one. Nothing. I was too exhausted to feel alarmed. I stepped over the threshold and spotted an envelope on the night stand. Inside was a piece of hotel stationery. On it was a long note. I sat down on the bed.

The note read:

"Hello, Ms. Davis. I'm with Victim Witness Services. I came with Lieutenant Grozny. He was very disappointed you weren't here. Your friend Betty Jackson used to be my mother's counselor and Mom loves her. I'm taking her back to our house for now. She can stay until you get here or for as long as she likes."

The woman had printed her name, phone number and address at the bottom of the page, and a few more words, "and the cat."

Ah, Betty was safe, Mange included. It came with a rush that I was even safe, for now. I kicked off my sport shoes and curled up on top of the bedspread in the middle of the king-sized bed. I pulled a pillow under my head. Reservoirs of tension drained from my mind and body. I think it was only second before I slept.

Loud noise woke me. Someone knocking. Where was I? I stumbled to the door in my socks and opened it before I remembered. Grozny didn't wait for an invitation. He pushed the door the rest of the way open and let himself in. A man I later knew as another plain-clothes officer entered behind him.

"Give me one good reason I shouldn't arrest you," Grozny said, taking a step toward me.

I backed up, reached behind me to put a hand on the night table. I said, "Because I have information you need, and I haven't done anything wrong. Give me one good reason I shouldn't lodge a complaint against Officer Benson--what he did to my dog, how he arrested me for nothing. There are other questions about him, too."

Lieutenant Grozny's eyes narrowed and the hint of a smile touched his thin lips. "The dog actually belongs to Kim Altaha, doesn't he?"

"Of course, but he was with me when...."

"You said you have information for me, Miss Davis, but you're asking the questions. You have quite an imagination and you obviously haven't read the morning paper."

"The paper?"

"Let's sit down."

I was stunned into silence. Had the newspaper already picked up news about little Buddy's kidnapping? We moved to the alcove with a round table and two chairs. I sat down, slowly. The other detective sat on the bed, casually crossed an ankle over his knee, took out a note book and pen, obviously prepared to listen and record.

Grozny said nothing but continued to stare at me. I asked, "So what's the news?"

"First, tell me what you think you know about Officer Benson."

"Why is that important? What else did he do besides traumatize Kim's dog?"

"I asked you the important question."

I said, "Benson was right there when I saw her body--Carrie Lougee's body. He yelled at me and said it was a crime scene. It couldn't have been more than ten or twelve minutes after I heard her scream. He got there so fast."

"That's right. I wouldn't tell you this, if someone in the department hadn't leaked it to a reporter. You may be the last one in town to know, Miss Davis. Officer Benson and Carrie were friends. Good friends. When she realized someone was trying to hurt her, she ran. While she was running, she took out her phone and pressed one key to speed dial Benson's private number, to ask for help. He followed procedure. He called dispatch and advised them he was on his way to Watson Woods."

I nodded. It made sense now. I said, "It was Garvin. Garvin Kastner. He kidnapped the baby, too." The conversation that followed was a long one. I was able to infer from the few additional details Grozny revealed that Kastner had been their primary suspect from the start. I interrupted our exchange long enough to retrieve my tote bag from the trunk of my car, the bag containing evidence of Kastner's thefts.

After the two detectives examined some of the records, and discussed what it meant, verbally beat the issue to death, in my opinion, I took out my phone and explained about the Fitbit. Grozny said he was familiar with the gadget. Data from one was admitted into evidence in a recent court case. He wanted to hold the phone to examine the app more closely. It felt like an intrusion to hand it over to him, but I did. While he looked at the record, a text message tone sounded. It was Kastner's exercise share message. I reached for it and quickly told Grozny what it was. We looked at it together, both our hands on the phone. Right now, Kastner's heart was racing as fast as possible for a person of his age. It was pounding away at one hundred and seventy beats per minute. Was he at Lynx Lake? What was happening?

***

Before I go back to Garvin, Chris, Kaska, Kim and Zayd at Lynx Lake--before I end the story, I need to go back to the very beginning, the Sunday morning ten days ago when Zayd and I entered High Meadows. I want to show you that day's events from Garvin Kastner's point of view. It's chilling. It may even seem inhuman. We need to stay with it in order to   understand.

Chapter Thirty-Four

Garvin Kastner, Betty Jackson and Carrie Lougee. Sunday

He didn't plan to kill her, but knew he would, with pleasure, if it was necessary. He had left the gun at home, but he could take care of her without it. Yesterday, Carrie had visited Betty when he wasn't there. Somehow, she had gotten a look at Betty's checkbook. Afterward, she called him to ask what he had been doing with Betty's finances. He could explain everything, he told her, and managed to calm her down. They agreed to meet today at a coffee shop. He called her at the last minute and told her he couldn't make it because Betty had made a mess in the kitchen that he needed to clean up. Ten minutes later, he called again, saying he had done the cleaning and now to get out of the house, wanted to take a walk in the woods to regain his composure. It wasn't safe to leave Betty alone for long, so would she come to him for their talk?

At eight-forty a.m. that cool May morning, they met at the cul-de-sac near the path into the woods. She wouldn't respond to his pleasantries. She demanded to know why Betty had made out so many checks to him, and why she had signed blank checks. He strolled into the trees while he talked. He was adept at this verbal sparring. He didn't give direct answers. He talked in circles. He asked her irrelevant questions, trying to confuse her or distract her from the topic.

She walked with him into the woods. Soon her questions became accusations. He enjoyed the debate. He denied, argued, and finally attempted to charm her. They walked for about ten minutes.

Suddenly, she wouldn't answer him. She stopped and held up both hands, palms outward.

He knew it was all or nothing. He had only one chance to turn her. He said, "Okay, here's what I'll do." He offered her a share of the old woman's money--half a million, with all the assets combined.

He recognized the look of disgust on her face. She turned to go. He grabbed her arm. She jerked loose, walked away. Fear emanated from her retreating figure, reached him in waves. He started after her. She turned and when she saw him coming, she screamed. It stirred something primitive in him.

When it was over, he knew he had to leave quickly, without being seen. Her screams might have drawn a witness. He was sure she hadn't had time to dial 911 on her phone. He had crushed it under his heel on the ground where it fell and now held the shattered remains in his hand. He would dispose of it, tend to any other unpleasant business--like clean up any specks of blood on his clothes and hands. Then his new life in this cute little cardboard cutout of a town would return to normal.

The incident--he named it that at once--was quickly stored in a special part of his mind reserved for such events. Not that he wanted to forget it. It would be a pleasing memory to retrieve, review, and relish. Until then it would remain in that special compartment in his brain he had labeled "what other people call it" or "what other people think of it."

As he had told Allie, he was fine with himself, demons and all. He was incapable of the emotion known as guilt, so out of necessity, he had constructed this unique realm of consciousness that provided him with full deniability. It simply didn't matter what other people called it or what other people thought of it. I was part of him; of course it was okay.

He emerged from the woods at a fast walk, then took to the sidewalk on Maple Street at a casual stroll. He saw no one else out and about. He reached the house in five or six minutes but stopped outside the back door to wash his hands and face at the hose bib.

He had just turned the knob when Betty opened the door. She wore a blue kimono over a gauzy nightgown. She held a hummingbird feeder. When she saw him, she stopped short. "Garvin, I didn't expect you back so soon."

He bent to his task.

"Garvin, is that blood on your hands?"

"Of course not."

She stepped off the concrete onto the grass and came closer. "It is blood! Where are you bleeding?"

He stood up, leaving the faucet on. "I am not bleeding."

"I see a spot on your face! What happened?" Her own face tightened into creases. Both hands went to her mouth. Sugar-water from the feeder splattered onto her neck. She looked at the feeder, then turned this way and that until she focused on the tree limb where it belonged. She moved with care to hang the feeder before she turned to him.

Kastner could not have predicted this complication with his aunt. She was demented but she wasn't stupid. She had never been stupid. He said, "I didn't want to mention it, but I found a dead fox on the path in the woods. I picked it up to throw in farther away, so no one else would stumble over it. That's all, Aunt Betty." Even as he said it, he knew the explanation was ridiculous, but it seemed to satisfy her. She wiped sugar water from her neck, turned and went back into the house.

In the bathroom, he looked in the mirror for traces of blood on his face that he might have missed, then inspected his clothing for spatters. Yes, he would have to throw them away, even the pricy blue jeans. He drew on clean clothes then stood at the closet, deciding which pair of boots to wear. A distant sound distracted him. A siren. Damn! Surely she hadn't been found this quickly! He had to know what was up. He told himself it was perfectly fine to be curious. Anyone would be. He went to his car and drove the short distance back to the cul-de-sac.

Days later, after the police interrogated him the second time, Kastner had an epiphany--how to turn the tables, send them in a different direction. He would make an anonymous call to the dick involved, Grozny, the detective with the beady eyes. Grozny would buy it.

From a pay phone in front of Wal-Mart, he informed Grozny that Chris and Carrie had been banging it. It stood to reason. His son's wife was pregnant, then out of commission after the baby. Carrie was available and not half-bad looking.

They bought it, of course, but that didn't take all the pressure off. The Davis woman, his son's therapist, questioned him but wouldn't answer shit for him in return. What had Chris told her? How much did Allie and the Indian, the young hottie, actually know? Kim wouldn't tell him. His best efforts to arrange a little pillow talk, so he could pull the information out of her that way, didn't work. He couldn't let it go.

He decided on a much riskier ploy using a few of his former skills, a little episode of breaking and entering. The file in Davis's office was enlightening. If Chris had whined to Allie about him, she hadn't written it down, but even that didn't answer all his questions. And for some reason, the squeeze from police   continued.   Then....

Chapter Thirty-Five

Wednesday morning around 7:00 a.m. Chris, Kaska, Kim and Zayd.

Kaska parked his SUV at the lot near the natural history museum by the lake. Chris opened the door and got out. Kaska did also. Chris questioned the older man with his eyes.

"I'm going with you," Kaska said.

"I can't ask you to do that."

"You didn't. I know this area, too. I can help you." His eyes held steady with those of the younger man. Neither moved, until Kaska gestured toward the woods and said, "Let's go."

Chris led the way. The lake was fifty yards to their left. Through close-growing oak, ponderosa pine and juniper, they saw the rising sun cast a sheen of tender pink and pale gold on the water's surface. Mallards feathered in green and blue floated near the shore, which was lined with both live trees and a few tall snags. While they watched, a large bird swooped into view, dove into the water and emerged with a fish in its beak. Chris stopped. "A bald eagle!"

Kaska shook his head *'no.'* He said, "Eagles catch fish in their talons. That's an osprey." Five minutes more into the forest, he asked Chris, "How are we going to find this trap, this spider-hole in the ground? Are there markers?"

"I remember a big gnarly tree with what looks like a face, just a few feet north of it."

"Ah. Probably an Arizona white oak. Lots of them have those features."

Chris said, "The one I remember has two big knots on the trunk and a slash under them." He pointed ahead. "Closer to those dead trees."

***

When Kim took my car and drove back to the lake, unknown to the two men, she parked in the restaurant parking lot. Then she and Zayd trotted down the winding path to the lakeshore. At a ninety degree angle from the men's position, they began the search for Kastner, unaware Chris and her father stalked Kastner from another vantage point.

Kim reached down to stroke Zayd's head, then unhooked his leash and told him '*sit*.' Removing her backpack, she placed the coiled leash inside and took out the double-bagged t-shirt Allie had found for her in Kastner's bathroom. Zayd's ears perked. His tail wagged. He shivered. He emitted a short, high pitched whine of anticipation, scarcely able to remain in his obedient *sit*. Kim lifted the soiled shirt from inside the bags and held it to his nose. He sniffed, whined, started to rise, then sat and sniffed again, waiting.

"Find!" she said.

He leapt to all fours, darted to the side, his nose to the ground, then turned back. He zig-zagged over the rough terrain, lifting his head for split-seconds to orient himself. Startled butterflies fluttered from cactus blooms. An Abert's squirrel sitting on a manzanita shrub dashed up a nearby pine tree. A great blue heron near the shore lifted its long, graceful wings to flee the sudden activity.

Kim watched and waited while the dog searched. Long minutes later, panting, he slowed, stopped and lifted his head to air scent in one direction then another. Nothing.

Inexplicably, or perhaps prompted by intuition, Kim's attention shifted toward her left, across the spillway to the east shore of the lake. She turned. "Zayd, come!" The top of the spillway was dry, a perfectly paved path to the other side. Zayd followed. A minute after they crossed the narrow walkway, he darted in front of her, air scented again, yelped and raced forward.

***

Garvin Kastner. Hiding the Trans Am so it couldn't be seen from the road was a bit tricky but he had figured it out ahead of time. He turned off onto an old logging road that wound through the forest, two faint tire tracks overgrown with seedlings and carpeted with pine needles. When the track turned sharply, the car was invisible from the road and he stopped. He'd have to leave the bitch here, of course, steal another ride not so eye-catching to make it to Phoenix. In Phoenix he would go to Sky Harbor Airport and from there, to Belize. His off-shore accounts, plump with at least part of the booty from his aunt's estate, would fund a busy, tropical lifestyle.

He reached the hole as the bottom curve of the sun's globe escaped the horizon's grasp to strike the lake. A chimera appeared, the illusion of a vast pool of liquid gold. He smiled. It was all going his way. He pulled dead leaves, branches and pine needles from the wooden plank covering the spider-hole, then lay on his stomach to lift out the items he had stashed. Everything but the rifle fit into his backpack. The pistol, the Smith and Wesson Four-Ten Governor stayed tucked under his belt at the small of his back.

He left the hole gaping without its camouflage roof. He stepped onto the deer trail perpendicular to the spillway. Faint sounds of movement on the forest floor behind him made him turn. Two figures, two men coming toward him. He recognized his son but not the other man. He brought the rifle to his shoulder, got off two shots. One man hit. A spurt of blood, the evidence. Then both men were down.

Back on the trail at a run, he didn't see the dog until it was almost on him, dark body, wolf-like eyes, silent, focused on him, the target, the prey. He started to raise the rifle. The dog was too close, coming too fast. He threw it down. He darted downhill toward the lake. He leaped at the low-hanging branch of a dead tree. The tall snag was bone-white, all the bark rotted away, a slippery climb. A barrier above gouged the top of his head, sticks and branches. It was a huge nest. Panicked, furious, he swung at it. Nestlings the size of small chickens raised their scrawny necks, uttering shrill cries, 'skreee.' Their mouths opened wide in expectation of food. He pulled the gun from the small of his back, struck the nest with it, struck again. Sticks and limbs loosened. On the third swing, most of the huge construction crumbled apart, then tumbled twelve feet to the ground. With it went the two nestlings.

The dog, that black hell-hound below, dodged the descending wreckage. Kastner aimed the hand gun at it, fired, and missed. He spotted the girl. He re-sighted on her. In the same second, a winged demon descended on him. Its beating wings buffeted him. Rank odors of blood and fish engulfed him. He saw only white feathers, an orange craw, eyes that pierced him with fear.

The eagle's beak struck him on the cheek, opening a three inch gash. He flailed at the thing, almost fell. He tried to shoot it, but the shot went wild. He was unbalanced, grabbed the nearest branch for support. The dead wood cracked, splintered. The gun flew out of his hand as he tumbled to the ground, arms flailing. On his back, he was dimly aware he was not badly hurt. He had fallen on the nest and the two chicks. His body was crushing theirs.

Another Valkyrie descended on him. Now there were two of them, screaming like howls of the dying, slashing at his cheeks, his scalp, stabbing and gouging his eyes. He heard and felt a sickening 'pop.' A liquid orb spilled down his cheek and off his chin. His arms wind-milled to ward off the eagles. No use. Scalding   pain.

Chapter Thirty-Six

When Kastner fell, Kim and her dog backed farther away from him and the eagles. The raptors continued to savage the man who lay on the ground on top of their dying chicks. The shrieks of man and eagles, the bloody mess that was Kastner's head and face shocked and sickened her. She picked up a tree limb and approached the carnage, yelling and waving the branch. The two raptors dodged and then refocused on the attack. She persisted. Zayd began to bark and charge at them. They finally rose to the top branch of the snag to look down at the devastation below.

For the last few minutes, Kim had been dimly aware of other humans present, men shouting, moving through the forest. A uniformed man pushed through the undergrowth toward her. When he spotted the bloody figure on the ground at her feet, he raised his long gun at her. She grabbed Zayd's collar and put her free hand in the air, palm toward him. He was one of a dozen law enforcers who had run toward the sounds of rifle and pistol shots, instead of away from them.

***

Garvin's Fitbit had launched the assault team that stormed Lynx Lake. Rather, it was what I told Grozny must be happening there, based on what the Fitbit showed, innocent people in danger, a killer trying to make a getaway. To my surprise, Grozny understood. We were finally on the same track, after the same result. He called out the assault team. The team's commander called the police chief, who arrived minutes after his officers, to take charge of the operation.

During the tactical operation, officers had arrested both Kim and Chris. They were transported to the booking facility for questioning. EMTs waited in ambulances in the parking lot for his all-clear signal. When it came, they carried away a man whose head and face resembled raw meat, and an older man with a bullet wound in his upper arm.

Later, we learned from Chris that Kim's father had leapt in front of Chris when Garvin shot at them. Chris had used his belt for a tourniquet on Kaska's arm and started to carry Kaska to safety before he gratefully surrendered the wounded man to the EMTs.

Police questioned my friend and my client for hours. I was there at the booking facility, making a fuss, I think, trying to explain that they were both heroes instead of criminals. After I asked Grozny to intervene, other detectives reviewed multiple sources of information that cleared them. Before the end of the same day, Kim and Chris gained their release.

It was over--but of course, not really over. I learned that Chris reunited with his wife and son that evening. They celebrated by going to bed, with Chris Junior, little Buddy, sleeping in the crib they moved beside their bed. I hope they had faith that Chris's recovery would be difficult but successful, worthy of every effort, every insight, every sacrifice. Because it was. That's how it turned out.

When law enforcement released Kim, she went straight to the hospital to be with her father, who was out of surgery and receiving his overdue kidney dialysis. The trauma he had just been through had changed something in his soul, he said. What he had just been through was the strangest adventure of his life, but it convinced him that a person may not know why he or she remains among the living, but they must trust in a higher wisdom beyond human understanding to set their Earthly life span. With that knowledge, he continued on dialysis until the end.

As for me, I was proud and happy that my meeting with Lieutenant Grozny launched the tactical operation that saved Kaska's life. My curiosity and amateur snooping in the events of the two previous weeks, along with my determined actions that followed, won the respect of the police lieutenant. In fact, we became--almost--friends.

Eventually, Grozny told me why Kastner was on their radar from the beginning. They had discovered and identified his telephone calls to Carrie the morning of her murder. Their investigation and pursuit of his son, Chris Aren, was part of their efforts to build a case against Kastner.

A grand jury indicted him for the murder of Carrie Lougee. Kastner's face was all but destroyed in the eagles' attack. They blinded one eye and plucked out the other. He died four days later, weakened by blood loss and a massive infection that spread to his brain.

***

Local and national news outlets, including social media, covered the story that began with the murder of an innocent woman in Watson Woods and ended with the killing of eaglets at Lynx Lake. The loss of the two birds did not seem quite as tragic as it would have when the raptors were still an endangered species, although public fondness for the iconic symbol of American freedom remained strong.

When police department attorneys concluded Kim Altaha, Chris Aren and I were not planning to sue the agency for false arrest, the department issued formal apologies. Several months later, Prescott Police gave Kim and Zayd an "Everyday Heroes" award. Media watchers and reporters and jumped on the story. TV and film producers made overtures for rights to tell it in their own way, attempting to sign both Kim and her dog. Kim refused. I was proud of her. She wanted only to do the job she valued, be with the man she loved and live life fully and well. She declined other attempts by the media to exploit Zayd, but she did allow an animal rescue organization to use his image for their fund raising campaign.

***

Betty, the almost-forgotten victim amid all the turmoil, endured fairly well all the disruptions and shocks of those weeks in May, due in part to my help. We decided a good option for both of us would be for me to move into her house, into the room Garvin Kastner had occupied. That's another story. I won't describe the hauling out of furniture, ripping up of carpet, savaging away every trace of him which had to precede my move. I was able to hire a care-giver to stay with Betty during the day, while I continued my counseling work. Betty's attorney, working with the Prescott police, recovered most of her financial assets that were stolen by Kastner.

On the last Sunday in May, early in the morning, I returned to High Meadows Park. I missed having Zayd by my side but the thought that he was with his partner Kim, able to do the volunteer search and rescue work they both loved, comforted me.

The garden was doing well, although it would be a few weeks more before I could harvest ripe tomatoes and peppers. I did pinch off a few sprigs of rosemary to flavor the roast chicken I would prepare for dinner. When I left the park, instead of going the short way home, I detoured through a different residential area, again admiring the comfortable homes and stable neighborhoods while I walked. Their aura of tranquility and permanence didn't move me, didn't draw my emotion as before. I still admired them, but saw them in a different light.

I also saw myself in a different light. In the past few weeks, I had defied authority by refusing to obey an order from the County Attorney, conspired with Kim and others to aid and abet a presumed suspect for murder, lied to police, snooped and plotted and connived.

A cooler breeze touched my face as I neared my new home, a simple pleasure for someone totally at peace with herself. I looked up to see clouds moving in, low and fast. The first drops of rain fell on my face like mist from a waterfall. Slowly, their size increased to droplets, then drops. Their erratic tempo of descent steadied to a heavy rhythm. I didn't quicken my pace and soon I was soaked. Still in no hurry, my feet sloshed and splashed in growing puddles. The sight of a lawn sprinkler sending its spray upward to meet the falling drops made me smile. A few cars passed by. I imagine the drivers thought I was crazy, walking as calmly as if sunshine warmed my shoulders. If I could, I would tell them I don't subscribe to the belief that I will melt in water, like the Wicked Witch of the West, or come down with my death-of-a-cold, like the delicate ladies of old.

A white SUV passed me for the second time, then the third. Abruptly it pulled over next to me. The driver rolled down his window and leaned toward me, holding out a red umbrella. I took it, smiled at him, blinking water out of my eyes. "Thank you! Where can I leave this to get it back to you?"

His face was round and pleasant. In the voice of a friendly conspirator, he said, "Oh, don't bother. My pleasure." He drove away. I unfurled the umbrella, ' it over my dripping head and shoulders and
~n.

###

Author's Message

Thank you for reading *A Killing at Lynx Lake.* If you enjoyed it, please write a review on Amazon.com. The instructions are easy to follow. All reviews help authors reach a larger audience.

If this is the first time you've read about Allie, Kim, Betty and Zayd the rescue dog, read their back story in *The Well* and *Apache Refuge,* books one and two of the Arizona Thriller Trilogy.

Regards,

Sharon Sterling

P.S. If you'd like to connect with me, go to my

web site: http://sharonsterling.net

Facebook page: Sharon Sterling Author

215

Made in the USA
Columbia, SC
30 August 2017